Praise for *Just In Case*

'A modern *Catcher in the Rye* . . . written with generosity
and warmth but also with an edgy, unpredictable intelligence'
– *The Times*

'Unusual and engrossing' – *Independent*

'Extraordinary' – *Observer*

'No one else writes the way Rosoff does – as if she's
thrown away the rules. I love her fizzy honesty, her
pluck, her way of untangling emotion through words'
– Julie Myerson

Books by Meg Rosoff

HOW I LIVE NOW

JUST IN CASE

WHAT I WAS

megrosoff.co.uk

What I Was

Praise for *How I Live Now*

'A crunchily perfect knock-out of a debut novel'
– *Guardian*

'This is a powerful novel: timeless and luminous'
– *Observer*

'That rare, rare thing, a first novel with a sustained,
magical and utterly faultless voice' – Mark Haddon,
author of *The Curious Incident of the Dog in
the Night-Time*

'Unforgettable . . . Rosoff achieves a remarkable feat'
– *Sunday Times*

'Gripping and powerful' – *Independent*

'Intense and startling . . . heartbreakingly romantic'
– *The Times*

'A wonderfully original voice' – *Mail on Sunday*

'Readers won't just read this book, they will let it
possess them' – *Sunday Telegraph*

'It already feels like a classic, in the sense that you
can't imagine a world without it' – *New Statesman*

'Fresh and original' – *Time Out*

MEG ROSOFF

What I Was

PENGUIN BOOKS

PENGUIN BOOKS

Published by the Penguin Group
Penguin Books Ltd, 80 Strand, London WC2R ORL, England
Penguin Group (USA) Inc., 375 Hudson Street, New York, New York 10014, USA
Penguin Group (Canada), 90 Eglinton Avenue East, Suite 700, Toronto, Ontario, Canada M4P 2Y3
(a division of Pearson Penguin Canada Inc.)
Penguin Ireland, 25 St Stephen's Green, Dublin 2, Ireland (a division of Penguin Books Ltd)
Penguin Group (Australia), 250 Camberwell Road, Camberwell, Victoria 3124, Australia
(a division of Pearson Australia Group Pty Ltd)
Penguin Books India Pvt Ltd, 11 Community Centre, Panchsheel Park, New Delhi – 110 017, India
Penguin Group (NZ), 67 Apollo Drive, Rosedale, North Shore 0632, New Zealand
(a division of Pearson New Zealand Ltd)
Penguin Books (South Africa) (Pty) Ltd, 24 Sturdee Avenue, Rosebank, Johannesburg 2196, South Africa

Penguin Books Ltd, Registered Offices: 80 Strand, London WC2R ORL, England

penguin.com

First published 2007
1

Text copyright © Meg Rosoff, 2007
Map copyright © David Atkinson, 2007

The moral right of the author has been asserted

Set in Sabon by Palimpsest Book Production Limited, Grangemouth, Stirlingshire
Made and printed in England by Clays Ltd, St Ives plc

British Library Cataloguing in Publication Data
A CIP catalogue record for this book is available from the British Library

hardback
ISBN: 978-0-141-38343-9

trade paperback
ISBN: 978-0-141-38392-7

www.greenpenguin.co.uk

Mixed Sources
Product group from well-managed
forests and other controlled sources
www.fsc.org Cert no. SA-COC-1592
© 1996 Forest Stewardship Council

Penguin Books is committed to a sustainable future
for our business, our readers and our planet.
The book in your hands is made from paper
certified by the Forest Stewardship Council.

*For my parents,
Lois Friedman and Chester Rosoff,
with love*

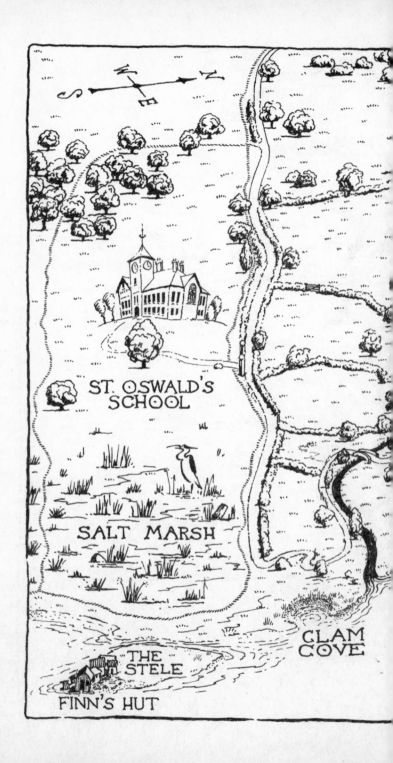

LOST
CITY

ROMAN
FORT

COAST ROAD

FINN'S
CLIFFS

I am a century old, an impossible age, and my brain has no anchor in the present. Instead it drifts, nearly always to the same shore.

Today, as most days, it is 1962. The year I discovered love.

I am sixteen years old.

1

Rule number one: Trust no one.

By the time we reached St Oswald's, fog had completely smothered the coast. Even this far inland, the mist was impenetrable; our white headlights merely illuminated the fact that we couldn't see. Hunched over the wheel, Father edged the car forward a few feet at a time. We might have driven off England and into the sea if not for a boy waving a torch in bored zigzags by the school entrance.

Father came to a halt in front of the main hall, set the brake, pulled my bag out of the boot, and turned to me in what he probably imagined was a soldierly manner.

'Well,' he said, 'this is it.'

This is what? I stared at the gloomy Victorian building and imagined those same words used by fathers sending their sons off into hopeless battle, up treacherous mountains, across the Russian steppes. They seemed particularly inappropriate here. All I could see was a depressed institution of secondary education suitably shrouded in fog. But I said nothing, having learnt a thing or two in sixteen years of carefully judged mediocrity, including the value of silence.

It was my father's idea that I attend St Oswald's, whose long history and low standards fitted his requirements exactly. He must have rejoiced that such a school existed – one that would accept his miserable failure of a son and attempt to transform him (me) into a useful member of society, a lawyer, say, or someone who worked in the City.

'It's time you sorted yourself out,' he said. 'You're nearly a man.' But a less true description could scarcely have been uttered. I was barely managing to get by as a boy.

My father shook hands with our welcoming committee as if he, not I, were matriculating, and a few moments of chat with head and housemaster ensued. Wasn't the weather . . . hadn't standards . . . next thing we know . . . one can only . . .

I stood by, half-listening, knowing the script by heart.

When we returned to the car, my father cleared his throat, gazed off into the middle distance, and suggested I take this opportunity to make amends for my last two educational disasters. And then, with a pessimistic handshake and a brief clasp of my shoulder, he was off.

A bored prefect led me away from the main school towards a collection of rectangular brick buildings arranged around a bleak little courtyard. In the misty darkness, my future home uncannily resembled a prison. As we entered Mogg House (Gordon Clifton-Mogg, housemaster), the weight of the nineteenth century settled around my shoulders like a shroud. Tall brick walls and narrow arched windows seemed designed to admit as little light and air as possible. The architect's philosophy was obvious: starve the human spirit, yes, but subtly, employing economies of dimension and scale. I could tell from here that the rooms would be dark all year round, freezing in winter, cramped and airless in summer. As I later discovered, St Oswald's specialized in architectural sadism – even the new science lab (pride of the establishment) featured brown glass and breeze-block walls dating from 1958, height of the ugly unfriendly architecture movement.

Up three flights of stairs and down a long featureless corridor we trudged. At the end, the older boy dumped my bag, pounded on the door and left without waiting for an answer. After a minute I was granted entry to a cramped dormitory room where three boys looked me over impassively, as if checking out a long shot in the paddock at Cheltenham.

There was a moment of silence.

'I'm Barrett,' said the blunt-featured one at last, producing a small black book from his pocket and pointing to the others in turn. 'Gibbon. And Reese.'

Reese giggled. Barrett made some notes in his little book, then turned to Gibbon. 'I give him two terms,' he said. 'You?'

Gibbon, tallest of the three, peered at me closely. For a moment I thought he might ask to see my teeth. He pulled two crisp pound notes out of an expensive calfskin wallet. 'Three terms,' he said.

I emptied all expression from my face, met and held his gecko eyes.

'Maybe four.'

'Choose,' said Barrett impatiently, pencil poised. He

squinted out from under a school cap pulled low over his face, like a bookmaker's visor.

'Three then.'

Barrett made a note in his book.

'I say four.' Reese dug into a pocket and pulled out a handful of coins, mainly pennies. He was the least impressive of the three, and seemed embarrassed by the ritual.

Barrett accepted the coins and looked up at me. 'You in?'

Was I *in* on a bet predicting the demise of my own academic career? Well, it certainly offered a variation on the usual welcome. I pushed past them, unpacked my bag into a metal trunk, made up my narrow bed with regulation starched sheets, burrowed down under the covers and went to sleep.

2

Rule number two: Keep something back.

I will tell you that I'm not one of those heroes who attracts admiration for his physical attributes. Picture a boy, small for his age, ears stuck at right angles to his head, hair the texture of straw and the colour of mouse. Mouth: tight. Eyes: wary, alert.

You might say that superficial flaws were not uncommon in boys my age, but in my experience this was untrue. Stretching left, right, up, down and diagonally in every St Oswald's class picture were boys of a more usual type – boys with strong jaws, straight noses and thick hair of definite colour; boys with long, straight limbs and bold, confident expressions; boys with skills, inborn talents, a genetically determined genius for politics or Latin or the law.

In such pictures, my face (blurry and unformed) always looked shifty and somewhat imbecilic, as if the flesh itself realized that the impression I was making was a bad one, even as the shutter clicked.

Did I mention that St Oswald's was my third school? The first two asked me (not entirely politely) to leave, due to the deplorable nature of my behaviour and grades. In my defence, I'd like to point out that my behaviour was not deplorable if by deplorable you mean rude, belligerent, violent and antisocial – setting fire to the library, stabbing or raping a teacher. By deplorable they meant 'less than dedicated to study', 'less than competent at writing essays', 'less than interesting to the head and board of governors'. Given my gentle failings, their assessment strikes me now as unnecessarily cruel, and makes me wonder how they labelled the student who opened fire with an AK-47 in the middle of chapel.

In fact, my lack of distinction was mainly restricted to photographs and schoolwork. When it came to opinions, I was (I am) like the sword of Zorro: swift, incisive, deadly. My opinions on the role of secondary education, for instance, are absolute. In my opinion, this school and its contemporaries were nothing more than cheap merchants of social status, selling an inflated sense of self-worth to middle-class boys of no particular merit.

I will, however, grant them something. Without the first school, I would not have ended up at the second. Without the second, I would not have attended St Oswald's. Without St Oswald's, I would not have met Finn.

Without Finn, there would be no story.

3

It all began on the coast of East Anglia, past the indentation where the River Ore ran salt and melted into the sea. There, a bit of land stuck out from the mainland, a small peninsula roughly shaped like a rat's nose. In maps (old maps) this peninsula was labelled The Stele, after a seventh-century commemorative stone marker, or stele, found very near to school property in 1825.

The letter my school sent to prospective parents contained a three-quarter page description of the area. Location was a selling point (*salt air contributes to strong lungs and clear minds*) and elegant italics explained how the stele was found half-buried in earth, the stone large and heavy and probably transported from Lindisfarne on the Northumbrian coast. Such markers were not uncommon in this part of the country, but this one boasted an excellent carved portrait of St Oswald, a seventh-century king of Britain, with the Anglo-Saxon equivalent of 'Oswald Was Here' carved on it. The stone itself is long gone, moved to the British Museum.

St Oswald's School for Boys, which you won't have heard of, was situated two miles inland. The school road ran between the A-road and the coast in a more or less straight line, with a footpath running parallel for most of its length. At the sea, the road turned left (north), while the footpath turned right (south). Following the footpath, you could reach The Stele in about twenty minutes – or at least you could reach the canal of deep water that separated it from the mainland. For only a few hours a day, when the tide was very low, the little peninsula could be accessed via a damp sand causeway. All around it, salt marsh and reed beds provided homes for nesting waders and waterfowl – oyster catchers, little terns, cormorants, gulls – and had once done the same for Roman, Saxon and Viking settlers.

A few miles and a million light years away was my home from home, Mogg House, a four-storey building with studies (tiny as tombs) on the bottom floor, communal dormitories in the middle, and bedrooms with living rooms on the floors above. Boys my age lived on the top floor in rooms designed for two, which now housed four, thanks to our bursar's desire to maximize revenues. Loos were located on the ground floor, and to this day I believe I retain exceptional bladder control thanks to the inconvenience of the conveniences. It was something we developed with time and practice, like proficiency in maths or arpeggio technique.

Despite the brutality of the coastal winters, we lived without heat. Warmth was considered antithetical to the development of the immune system and we were expected to possess an almost superhuman tolerance for cold. On a positive note, the conditions at my previous school – situated two hundred miles further north – had been worse. There, we kept warm in winter by sleeping in our clothes, in woollen jerseys, socks and trousers with pyjamas layered on top, and awoke most mornings to banks of snow under the open windows and ice in the toilets.

At St Oswald's, we fell out of bed at the sound of a bell, buttoned a clean collar (if we had one) on to our shirts, pulled on yesterday's underwear, flannel trousers, socks and heavy black shoes, and headed downstairs for a breakfast of grey porridge and cold toast. Post-war rationing had finished eight years before, but the habit of mean, depressing food lingered in school kitchens throughout the land. After breakfast came chapel, then five lessons on the trot without a break, followed by lunch (pink sausages, green liver, brown stew, cabbage boiled to stinking transparency), followed by an afternoon dedicated to sport or the tedium of cadet parade, followed by supper, followed by prep, followed by bed.

Beneath this relatively straightforward schedule lurked the shady regions of school life where the real dramas were played out, where elaborate hierarchies established life's winners and losers, ranking each carefully according to the ill-defined caste system of school life. As in the outside world, social mobility barely existed; one's status at the start determined whether life would be filled with misery or triumph. I don't recall any boy improving his lot significantly in the course of his school years, though perhaps memory fails me.

'Oi, you!'

Three days in, I emerged from my own thoughts to meet the gaze of an imperious Upper Sixth.

'*You!*'

Yes, I sighed inwardly. *Me*.

'What's that?' He pointed to the bottom button of my school blazer.

It's a woodpecker, you creeping maggot.

He reached over with calm deliberation and tore the button off. It's worth noting that this required considerable effort. And left a large hole.

'*Un*buttoned,' he spat. 'Understood?'

I stared.

'The correct answer, scum, is *Yes, sir*.'

'Yes, sir.' I had learnt to imbue a lack of sarcasm with infinite subtlety.

He turned on his heel and stalked off, while I scrabbled in the grass for my button. I felt no particular shame, having encountered dozens of chippy little fascists in my time, but continued to wonder at their delusions.

Our world revolved around school rules, rules as mysterious and arcane as the murkier corners of a papal cabal. Bottom button of blazer open or not, left hand in pocket or not, diagonal or straight crossing of the courtyard, running or walking on the lawn, books in right hand or left, blue ink or black, cap tipped forward or back. There was no crib sheet, no list to consult, no house book embossed *Rules*. Regulations merely existed, bobbing to the surface of school life like turds. We took their randomness, their rigidity, their sheer number, for granted and we obeyed because they were there, because we were newer or younger or weaker than the enforcers, because to fill our heads with more meaningful information might require the use of our critical faculties. Which would lead to doubts about the whole system. Which would lead to social and economic collapse and the end of life as we knew it.

It was easier just to get on with it.

Let me be clear: many boys (popular, clever, athletic) had a perfectly happy time at St Oswald's; I simply was not one of them. And yet I had certain attributes – a face that hid emotion, a healthy contempt for fair play – that served me well. I was not destined for glittering prizes, but I was not without qualities.

Our lessons took place beneath the draughty high ceilings of the main school building, always accompanied by the random clatter and crash of nineteenth-century plumbing. Day after day, I sat with an earnest but uncomprehending look on my face, knowing that it was exactly this expression that made teachers skip to the boy on my left. They hated explaining things over and over – it bored them, caused them to despise their lives.

Despite (or perhaps because of) the depressing familiarity of these conditions, I settled into St Oswald's at once.

4

One of the more notable facts about the stretch of coastline I have just described is that it is sinking at great speed.

This is the sort of fact about which it has become fashionable to panic in the middle of the twenty-first century, when nearly everyone agrees that our planet is on its last legs, but it has been true of this stretch of land for at least a thousand years. In contrast, the opposite coast in Wales is rising, which suggests that all of England is slowly tipping into the sea. Once the eastern coast sinks low enough and the western rises high enough, the entire country will slip gently under water in a flurry of bubbles and formal protests from the House of Lords. I greatly look forward to this gentle slipping into oblivion and believe it will do our nation no end of good.

Back then I might not have agreed. For one thing, I was less interested in geological catastrophe. For another, my contemporaries and I tended to view the future as a vast blank slate on which to write our own version of human history. But all this took a back seat to the real work that occupied each day – perfecting our lines for the drama of school life. It was important to be able to perform them without thinking – the not talking back, the respectful dipping of the head to teachers, the unsarcastic 'sir', the stepping aside for bigger boys.

I rarely thought about the schools I'd left behind; whatever impression they had made had been all bad. Getting ejected from the first had been effortless, requiring nothing more than an enthusiastic disdain for deadlines and games. Even without much of a reputation to uphold, they were pleased to see me go.

Expulsion from the second required slightly more effort, and the help of materials readily available from any school chemistry lab.

It occurred to me, however, that falling out of favour with St Oswald's (which specialized in low expectations) might be more difficult. Even the teaching staff, a ragtag bunch of cripples and psychological refugees, appeared to have few prospects elsewhere. Mr Barnes, a victim of shell shock with a prosthetic bottom and one eye, taught history. He had occasional good days during which he spoke with almost thrilling animation about battles and treaties and doomed royal successions, but the rest of the time he merely sat at the front of the class and stared at his hands. From motives having nothing to do with compassion we left him alone on his black days, tiptoeing out so that his classroom echoed with silence by the time the bell rang.

Thomas Thomas, a refugee from All Souls, Oxford, with a stutter and lofty ideals, attempted fruitlessly to seduce our souls with the poetry of Wordsworth and Keats. Even without the idiotic name he'd have been branded a victim;

15

with it, of course, he was doomed. We all knew his type: tall, dreamy and peevish, author of an unfinished novel destined to remain unfinished forever. It was easy to make him weep with frustration until he got the hang of school life, at which point (despite his aesthete tendencies and long white hands) he became our year's most enthusiastic applier of the cane.

M. Markel was always willing to set translations aside to recount his experiences with the maquisards, his comrades in the French resistance. We adored tales of torture and self-sacrifice under Vichy rule, but never heard one through to the end. The stories inflamed his passions to such a degree that, partway in, he would lapse into the impenetrable Basque patois of his youth.

The rest barely deserve mention. Mr Brandt (dull). Mr Lindsay (effeminate). Mr Harper (hairpiece, vain). Last, and least, was the dreaded Mr Beeson, headmaster (thick), who also taught RE. It's not that we thought we deserved a Mr Chips-type head (kindly, bespectacled, inspiring), but Mr Beeson barely topped five foot two, had the ruddy, unimaginative face of a butcher's apprentice, and cherished a private passion for Napoleonic battle re-enactments that far exceeded any interest he had in the teaching profession. Rumour had it that he had gained the post due to the unfortunate shortage of candidates in the years following the war. The fact that his knowledge of Latin and Greek seemed scarcely better than our own bore this out.

Have I forgotten to mention sport? Daily drilling in cricket or rugby took place under the relentless eye of Mr Parkhouse, who was a fiend for what he called 'conditioning'.

This entailed long runs across the muddy countryside on days when weather conditions prevented actual games. I can still hear the dull thud of all those feet, more than eighty at a time, propelled by sweaty thighs and wildly swinging arms, clambering through hedges and over stiles, too tired to express resentment but not too tired to feel it. To vary the routine we sometimes ran along the beach, panting along the damp sand in twos and threes until cramp or insurrection put an end to forward motion.

It is always Reese I think of when remembering these runs. He had taken to seeking me out, trailing me like a shadow, mistaking the person least interested in tormenting him for a friend. He had a disturbing tendency to pop up in exactly the place I least expected him to be, tangling my feet like a jungle snare, and most of the time all I wanted was to shake him off.

This combination of unwanted exercise and unwelcome company occasionally caused me to call a halt to the entire proceedings – once I lay flat behind a stand of trees, another time I crouched among the reeds until the thundering mass of boys disappeared from view. At those times, I felt a profound sense of release as I wandered back, admiring the mackerel sky and the soft silent swoop of owls.

This particular September morning was warm and intermittently sunny. Gold and purple heather set the marshes ablaze, and beyond lay the dark green surface of the sea. The low tide had created a long stretch of clear sand between the beach and The Stele, and Mr Parkhouse led us out on to the causeway at a brisk gallop. My breath, hoarse and loud, drowned the outraged calls of shore birds. Ahead was a small group of abandoned fishermen's shacks, mostly locked up and rotting with blacked-out windows. As we rounded the point, a feeling that irreparable damage had been done to my Achilles tendon made it clear that I should sit down, and I took advantage of the first shack to disappear from view.

As the rest of the boys ran on, Reese jogged on the spot, his desperate smile twisted into an unintentional leer. 'What you doing?'

'Bugger off,' I said. He turned beet red and legged it.

A dreamy silence settled on the spot. I lay slumped against the shack watching the soft rise and fall of waves, silencing my own breathing until there was no sound and nothing left in the world except sand and sea and sky. After a few minutes, the cloud cover gave way to a burst of brilliant sunlight and the slow dull sea leapt with diamonds.

The voice when it came was clear, oddly inflected, not unfriendly.

'What are you doing here?'

I looked up, startled. In front of me stood a person about my own age, with black eyes and a quizzical expression. He was slim, slightly taller than average and barefoot, his thick dark hair unfashionably shaggy. A heavy, old-fashioned fisherman's sweater topped baggy long shorts, chopped down from trousers and rolled.

He looked impossibly familiar, like a fantasy version of myself, with the face I had always hoped would look back at me from a mirror. The bright, flickering quality of his skin reminded me of the surface of the sea. He was almost unbearably beautiful and I had to turn away, overcome with pleasure and longing and a realization of life's desperate unfairness.

'I'm sorry,' I managed to stutter, pulling myself to my feet.

He gazed at me, taking in the exposed, blue-white schoolboy flesh, the stiff cotton shorts, the aertex vest plastered with sweat. From behind him a small grey cat gazed, its tail erect and twitching, as if testing the atmosphere for spies. Both looked, and neither shouted at me to leave. I took this as encouragement.

'I don't suppose I might bother you for –' I fought for an excuse, any reason to stay – 'a drink?'

The boy hesitated, reluctant rather than unsure, then shrugged, turned, and disappeared into the little shack. The cat stalked behind him, crossing one delicate paw in front of the other as he went. I followed, delighted and amazed by this unexpected turn of events. Compared to the beautiful boy and the cat I felt scruffy and crass, but I didn't mind, being not unused to scraping dignity out of pathos.

It took a moment for my eyes to adjust to the interior of the hut. There were only two rooms: a tiny sitting room at the front facing the sea and an equally small kitchen overlooking the reed beds. Flattened, nearly colourless rugs covered rough pine boards, and the chipped remnants of a once-fine set of china sat neatly on wooden shelves in the kitchen. Two smallish front windows opened on to sweeping views of the sea. Across the room, a narrow staircase led to what I assumed was a sleeping loft; a shallow pitched roof indicated that the space would be cramped. Beneath the stairs, a cupboard closed with a worn wooden latch. Simply framed photographs hung in uneven intervals on the wall above the staircase: a bearded man with a weathered face. A portrait of a young woman. A fishing boat. A shire horse.

All black and white. All decades old.

The low, banked fire in the iron stove threw off enough heat to make the hut feel warm and comforting as soup. Settled in front of the stove, the cat never took its eyes off me.

'You can sit if you like,' said the boy in a slightly stilted voice, as if he didn't speak English fluently or perhaps had lost the habit of speaking. He poured water from a large metal tin into a kettle and placed it on one of the hotplates.

I thought of the dreary Victorian schoolrooms of St Oswald's, of the freezing brick dormitories, of my parents' home with its gloomy semi-rural respectability. This place was unassuming and intimate, its spirit soft, worn and warmed by decades of use. It was as if I had fallen through a small tear in the universe, down the rabbit hole, into some idealized version of This Boy's Life.

Remembering what I had in the way of manners, I gave the boy my name and he didn't flinch – a rare enough reaction, and one I appreciated. Panic began to overtake me at the thought of having to drink my cup of tea and return to the reality of school food and school rules and school life. I sat, photographing the scene with my eyes and looking around for signs that the boy lived here with a grown-up of some description. The hut was very small, but also very tidy. The floors were free of sand, and there were none of the usual cheery beach relics crowded on to window sills. The cotton rugs, though worn, were immaculate. A large pyramid of wood had been stacked neatly beside the stove.

Not a detail out of place.

The boy returned to the little sitting room carrying a teacup with roses on it. 'It's black,' he said, handing me the tea, with no apparent desire to know if that would do.

'Thank you.' I raised the cup and gulped a hot mouthful. 'Do you live here alone?'

He did not welcome questions, this much was clear. Without answering, he turned back to the kitchen, followed by the cat. I waited for him to volunteer an explanation, but it didn't come so I jabbered instead, uncomfortable with silence.

'I'm at St Oswald's, a boarder. It's diabolical,' I said, in an effort to prove somehow that I was *on his side*. 'I hate studying and I'm no good at sport. It's cold all the time and the food is inedible. It's the most idiotic waste of time.' I looked up from my tea, anxious for sympathy. 'And money.'

He appeared not to be listening.

'Do you have a name?' I asked.

'Finn,' said the boy.

'Nice to meet you, Finn.'

I finished my tea slowly, but once it was gone could

think of no reason to stay. 'I'd better go then,' I said, with what sounded even to me like a lack of conviction.

'Goodbye,' Finn said and I felt like weeping.

Outside, I turned to wave, but Finn had already shut the door on our encounter. Back at school I'd missed breakfast, chapel, and the beginning of Latin. Which meant detention and fifty extra lines.

And bothered me not at all.

5

It was nearly a month before I saw Finn again. By means of careful questioning I uncovered rumours of a boy who lived by himself on the coast, but no one I asked seemed terribly interested in the story. If he existed he was probably desperately poor, on the dole, with an alcoholic mother who showed up occasionally and knocked him about. The hut probably stank. It was, in other words, not the sort of story that would interest my contemporaries, involving as it did poverty, misery, deprivation.

This pleased me. Finn was my fantasy and I didn't feel inclined to share.

Please don't get the wrong impression from my use of the word 'fantasy'. I didn't long to see him *in that way*. It wasn't even that I longed to *see* him so much as to *be* him, to escape the depressed sighs of my teachers, those exalted judges of my unexalted little life.

'Not an athlete,' sighed Mr Parkhouse. 'Not a student either,' sighed my Latin, maths, geography, French, English and RE masters.

And yet I wasn't quite ready to resign myself to the existence they imagined for me: the minor public school boy with the minor job, minor wife, minor life. I could see by their expressions that they had me pegged as the bank manager who never gets promoted, the accountant who can't afford to take the wife and children abroad, or even (imagine the horror) a sales person of some description – in advertising, perhaps, or insurance.

The truly frightening thing was that if you stared into enough eyes and saw enough of the same opinion staring back at you, you began to imagine that they might be right. What did I know, after all? My experience of the world came from comics and detective stories and Hitchcock films starring American actresses with stiff blonde hair. The rest of the time I spent staring at teachers or out of windows, or at the obscene scribbles on lavatory walls. Despite my exquisitely honed indifference, my life telescoped down to a few sad little desires: to have second helpings of food, to wear clothes that didn't itch or cause undue humiliation, to be left alone.

Twenty-four days after my first encounter with Finn I found myself on the beach again at low tide, this time on an unseasonably cold October day. As Mr Parkhouse led the stampede past the fishing huts, I could see smoke rising from Finn's chimney. It curled languidly, spelling out words of welcome against the bright grey sky.

Come in, it said. And, *It's warm . . .*

Reese matched me stride for stride, vigilant, ubiquitous. My bad luck charm.

'Meet you later,' I hissed, nodding him off in the direction of our fellow runners. He hesitated, reluctant, but eventually disappeared round the point with the rest of the class.

This time, although I sat and sat (ostensibly getting my breath back), Finn did not make an appearance. I turned myself into a stone on the beach, inanimate and invisible, ticking off the minutes in my head, wondering how long I could wait, so overcome with disappointment I might have cried. The thought of not standing once more in that room by the sea was too much to bear.

It was cold. My clothes were clammy with sweat and I shivered. There was nothing for it but to stand up, hold my breath and rap on the door. Once. Twice. Nothing. And then suddenly he was there, not inside the hut but appearing from the dunes beyond, eyes clear, walk graceful, smiling a little as if he might actually be glad to see me.

Relief rendered me speechless.

He said nothing, but reached round and opened the door for me, the gesture proprietary and still accompanied by a smile. It was not a big smile, not particularly bold or polite or ironic or glib, not asking for anything or offering anything, not stingy or careless, not, in short, like any smile I had ever experienced before. But such a smile! You could burn a hole in the world with that smile.

'Come in,' he said.

The tiny hut felt over-warm after my run and the fire caused little waves of steam to rise from my armpits and crotch. I talked while Finn made tea, spinning a mix of half-truths and blatant lies about life at St Oswald's. About the Latin master, mean and miserable, who beat us relentlessly and forced us to perform indecent acts after lessons. About the rats that nested in our shoes at night and had to be ejected snarling and squealing each morning. About the food, greyish meat in brownish sauce, the tasteless purple-grey puddings, the vegetables cooked unto mush (these things, at least, were true).

'It's vile,' I sighed. 'Torture by nutrition.'

Finn laughed at that, and I felt a tiny surge of triumph: I was Scheherazade, desperate to keep him amused.

He stirred the tea in an old brown teapot, poured it out black like last time, and handed me a cup. I perched on my bench and he sat on a painted wooden chair pulled from beside the stove. For the first time in weeks I relaxed, despite the fact that the only evidence I had for his friendship was that he hadn't yet asked me to leave. And once again, sitting in that warm room, I was swept by desire – to escape the dull tyranny of everyday life and live here, by the sea.

To be Finn.

I imagined simply disappearing. After a desultory search of the marshes, the school would give me up as a bad episode in an otherwise sterling history of mediocre achievement, inform my parents that I had perished in a freak boating accident or been struck by lightning and reduced to ash. There would be a few tears on the home front, yes, but they would forget me quickly and get on with their lives. It would be better for all concerned.

For me, particularly.

As my clothes dried and the tea warmed my insides, Finn stood up and began adding wood to the fire. With his back to me I found the courage to pick up the interrogation where I'd left it nearly a month ago.

'Do you live here alone?'

26

Once again he said nothing, but his lack of a denial proved the point in my eyes.

'But *everyone* has at least one parent.' Having said this, it occurred to me that perhaps Finn didn't. He might have been a product of spontaneous generation or emerged from the sea like Venus. Neither would particularly have surprised me.

I persisted. 'A relative?'

He merely shrugged. There was a note of finality in the gesture, and I didn't dare ask my next question, namely: *How on earth have you managed to live alone in a state of perfect grace, away from the local authority and the endless stream of oppressors who populate every minute of every normal life?* Although we were taught to be proud of living in this great parliamentary democracy, the civil servants who ran it were a fearsome bunch, a nameless mass of people with jobs (police, social workers, record-keepers, teachers, councilmen) whose sole purpose was to keep everyone shuffling from birth to death in a nice orderly queue. Surely some social service record had been passed to the local constabulary bearing a huge black question mark beside the name of Finn, and the scrawled words *Why isn't this boy in school?*

I looked around the little hut, at the tidy crammed bookcases, the framed painting of a ship, at the bench under the window with its thin mattress and faded striped blankets.

'But how do you live?'

He looked at me, uncomprehending.

Wasn't it obvious? 'Money. Food.'

'I work in the market, hauling boxes.'

'But,' I said, trying to prevent my voice from becoming querulous, 'but what about *school*?'

My outrage made him smile. That smile.

'I don't go.'

'*You don't go?*'

He looked at me mildly. 'No one knows I exist. My birth was never registered.'

Never registered? What a brilliant start in life! Finn not only had no parents, lived alone, didn't go to school, but according to the government, *he didn't actually exist*. I couldn't believe my ears. The area was rural but not that rural. It seemed impossible that here, in this modern twentieth-century state dedicated to the improvement of all its citizens by means of relentless conformity and hard graft, a boy could simply slip through the holes of the social net.

Envy was not nearly strong enough to describe what I felt.

I wanted to reassure him (though he didn't seem to require reassurance) that I would do everything in my power to keep the secret of his precarious existence. Even the little I knew about Finn convinced me that he was vulnerable to capture and dissection by well-meaning officials. Without conscience, they would pack him off to some bleak Dickensian children's home where he would be bullied, buggered, humiliated, and eventually found hanging from an improvised noose in his miserable cheerless room.

I didn't know much, but I knew that much.

Another dozen questions required answers, but before I could speak again Finn asked if I had any plans to return to school. I took it as a request and left.

As he shut the door behind me, I caught a glimpse of his face. It was inscrutable, composed. Perfect.

Rule number three: Not everyone is subject to rules.

Reese was waiting for me in our rooms, expectant and eager for the confidences I'd already forgotten promising.

'So?' He sat up like a trained squirrel, eyes glittering with excitement.

'So, what?' I was already late for history.

'You said . . .'

The penny dropped. 'I just stopped for a piss, Reese. That's all.'

His face fell. 'But . . . what about that boy?'

Collecting books and papers, pulling on my shoes, I continued to ignore him.

'I *saw* him, you know.'

'Clever old you,' I said, and left the room. His habitual wretchedness left me cold back then, as so much of human weakness did.

6

It's a strange sensation to live inside another person's life, to wonder all the time what he's doing, or thinking, or feeling. I wondered if Finn ever thought about me, if he ever looked over his shoulder to see if I had crossed the sand to visit him. I would like to have spent every minute of my life doing just that, but of course I couldn't. I had some pride, after all.

Instead, I stalked him.

I caught the bus into town after school, avoiding the sweet shop and off-licence where all normal schoolboys congregated, and wandered over to the market instead. It was a big town and the stalls ran off the high street for half a mile, down a long narrow road that ended at the fish market. The imposing marble building with the dolphin carved into the balustrade was still in use, but had seen better days. It looked tattered and sad, its tall windows opaque with grime. The marble gutters beside it held pools of bloody fish entrails and it stank.

At the high street end of the market, stalls sold dresses, men's socks and – irresistible and repellent at once – ladies' support garments. They were ugly beige with a surgical air and stoutly constructed, as if designed to conceal unpleasant truths about marriage. Kitchen goods were next, steel teapots and cheap tin saucepans, heavy china plates with red marks above the makers' names to indicate rejected stock. Then the fabrics: great bolts of rough grey suiting made from wool mixed with waste cellulose that would be hell to wear. Further down the road the domestic products gave way to carefully composed pyramids of fruit and veg. It being October, that meant piles of dusty beetroot, huge cauliflowers, cabbages and great wooden bins of runner beans. In two months it would all change – to parsnips, turnips, carrots and spuds.

Nothing about this market set it apart from ten thousand identical others scattered throughout England, but something of the noise and chaos excited me nonetheless. If I squinted to block out the shiny gadgets and trinkets, I could easily imagine myself a century or two earlier in a scene from Hogarth or Daumier. The faces certainly wouldn't have changed since then – the broken veins, bulbous noses and crafty eyes lifted straight out of *A Rake's Progress*.

I stood for a minute, just taking in the colour and noise and the great clamouring chaotic bulk of humanity all busy with everyday tasks. At school we lived with so much order and ritual and so little contact with real life that we might as well have been high-security prisoners or Trappist monks. There were no girls, no pets, no harried shouting fathers or sentimental doting mothers, no old people or babies, no sisters to pick up from ballet lessons, no dogs to walk or cats to feed, no heaps of bills arriving in the post each morning. As boarders, our basic needs were fulfilled, our brains and bodies stuffed full of texts and truths, but we were desperately, terminally, catastrophically starved of real life.

I looked for Finn.

He was there all right, near the end – his outline instantly recognizable among the broad-shouldered, raw-boned race of market vendors. He had his back to me, hauling boxes off a stack and packing them into the back of a van. A hard-faced stump of a woman watched him work, occasionally indicating which set of boxes went where. She had a kerchief tied round her neck and every few seconds scanned the market with quick, noticing eyes.

I wasn't in the mood to be noticed, and the market was already starting to thin, so I turned back and walked away from them, past the flowered nightdresses and cheap fabrics, back towards the high street. I paused at the butcher's where a sign reading *Fresh Meat* belied the fact that something (everything) smelled of death. Flies had colonized a cow's shin, and six glassy eyes stared sightlessly out of a trio of gently rotting sheep's heads. I shuddered and moved on.

At the top of the narrow street, there was nothing to do but head back. A few harried, last-minute shoppers bought bruised apples and onions from stallholders anxious to pack up and be off. I walked slowly, and this time he saw me from a distance and skipped a beat in the rhythm of stacking to look again and to steal a glance over at his employer. She had seen me too, though it hardly took a genius to pick a St Oswald's boy out of this particular crowd. Schoolboys weren't usually interested in mops and vegetables, and in my ugly grey-and-blue uniform I stood out among the housewives like a stoat in a pram.

I approached, failing to appear casual.

Finn collected his coat while the stump-woman unzipped a money belt that hung round the rolling slabs of her midsection and pulled out a few notes. I turned away out of a sort of modesty, or perhaps it was embarrassment on Finn's behalf. But really I wanted to stare at the exotic transaction, the exchange of work for money. Money in my world meant tuition cheques sealed in discreet white envelopes.

Finn disappeared for a moment behind the stall and reappeared with two bulging bags – I could see potatoes and carrots sticking out of one and in the other, a small pineapple, rare as an African parrot.

'Come on,' he said, as if I picked him up at the market every Thursday. I fell in, half a step behind and to his left, grateful and obedient as a hound.

He stopped at the baker's and bought a loaf of brown bread. As the owner bagged it and counted out his change, I cast about, desperate for an offering worthy of my devotion. In what I imagined was a grand gesture, I pointed to the most elaborate cake in the case – an absurd pink-and-white confection decorated with roses and piped icing – not noticing until it was too late that it was a christening cake complete with pink sugar cherub in the centre. I watched in horror as the woman's assistant, or perhaps it was her daughter, made a great show of placing the cake in a box and tying it with string. Finn glanced at me, bemused, as I handed over the money and accepted the vile thing, wishing above all wishes that time might reverse and release me from my shame.

It began to hail. We hunched our shoulders and huddled into our coats, me in my regulation school topcoat, Finn in a canvas jacket that didn't look very warm, neither of us with gloves. Exhaling white puffs of condensation, we hurried along, our footsteps hollow in the narrow cobblestone streets. It was dark and cold and almost everyone was indoors. On each side of the narrow street, cottages leant in towards us, leaking murmuring voices and small slivers of golden light. I felt like a moth, drawn to the cosy rooms beyond the shutters and curtains, rooms crammed with figurines and ugly suites of furniture where red-faced men and women watched the telly and mongrel collies snored. Smoke from a hundred coal fires poured out of chimneys and swirled around us in the frigid air. I held the cake stiffly behind my back, wondering if I could leave it on someone's doorstep, and lengthened my stride so my footsteps merged with Finn's.

It wasn't until we were out of town that he spoke. 'Shouldn't you be at school?'

I stopped, eyes wide. 'That's rich coming from you.'

He kept walking, and I skipped to catch up. 'I've given up. Nothing left to learn.'

He turned to gauge my expression, and one side of his mouth twitched up in amusement.

We didn't speak again till we reached the school gates. I hesitated, not knowing how to broach the subject of coming another time to the hut. Finn waited, silent, until

34

finally I thrust the cake at him, muttered goodbye and strode off with an unnaturally long and manly gait invented on the spot to impress.

When I finally had the courage to look back, he had vanished.

7

The featureless trundle of my existence began to change. At the time, I didn't have the insight to wonder at the transient nature of despair, but now I'm older I've seen how little it takes to turn a person's life around for better or for worse. An event will do, or an idea. Another person. An idea of a person.

In our cramped dormitory with its newspaper photos of film stars and football heroes stuck to every crumbling surface, I plotted my new life in private – insofar as privacy was available.

'Where've you been?' Reese, eager as ever.

'Prague.' I didn't look up, nor had to. Gibbon made a rude gesture to Barrett who suppressed a snort of derision. I shut my eyes and turned all three into voles.

A small paper bag launched by Gibbon flew through the air and landed heavily on my bed, splitting to release a smell of decay and a long rubbery tail. I picked it up gingerly and tossed it into the corridor, aiming for another door as the stooges howled with delight. The following morning I rose before dawn, removed that week's translations from Gibbon's exercise book, padded silently down five flights of stairs to the toilets, put the paper to good use, flushed and returned to bed. Between five and six I slept like a baby.

The next afternoon had been reserved for my half-term interview, *to gauge the progress of new boys in a manner consistent with our reputation for pastoral care.* I answered all questions in a manner designed to satisfy Clifton-Mogg that I was doing as well as could be expected. He nodded his head absently while I listed the myriad unpleasant episodes that had occurred during my first six weeks at school, and sent a note off to my parents with the words *he's settling in nicely*, written for perhaps the ten-thousandth time in his long and colourless career.

Actually, I was settling *out* nicely.

Two days after my third encounter with Finn, I caught the school shuttle into town after class.

I bought a tide chart at the newsagent's, then concentrated on squandering a month's hoarded pocket money on supplies. According to my chart, the tide would be lowest at 4 p.m., so I caught the bus back to school, waited at the gate until everyone had dispersed, and then set off. Except for the afternoon shuttle to town, we were in theory only allowed to leave school property with a written exeat from our housemaster. St Oswald's had not yet erected machine-gun towers and searchlights, however, so in practice the rule was nearly impossible to enforce.

Wary of the road, I chose the footpath that ran parallel, hidden behind a row of trees. It was bitterly cold and nearly dark by the time I reached the beach. The tide chart had actually worked, and I crossed the causeway on damp sand by the last pink streaks of evening light. I reckoned I had a couple of clear hours to hang around before the crossing flooded again.

It was impossible not to stumble in the gloom and I arrived at Finn's hut with the bottoms of my grey school trousers soaked. No light was visible within. I knocked, looking out to sea as I waited for an answer, a little spooked by the loneliness of the place and the hollow crash of the waves. The sky was a uniform grey and bled seamlessly into the sea at an invisible horizon. There was no up, no down, no past or future. Aside from the far-off ghost of a coal boat chugging its way from Newcastle, I could have placed myself in the seventeenth century, or the seventh. No conurbation glowed orange in the sky, no traffic boomed, no street lamps shone. I remembered what I'd read about the stele that was found nearby, and wondered about the men who transported it from Northumberland, how they had lifted the heavy stone off their boat, carried it inland and set it upright to honour St Oswald. I imagined their boats tethered to shore, fires lit beside hastily constructed huts, fat stars overhead. Their proximity spooked me, their lives suddenly as real as mine. At my feet I might find the remains of Saxon cooking pots and animal bones, traces of woollen clothing.

I felt a momentary urge to leap into the sea and swim free of the present.

No answer.

I knocked again, louder this time. How could he not be here? And what would I do now? I stood, silent, for a long moment and then as quietly as possible squeezed the latch and opened the door.

'Finn?' My voice wouldn't rise above a whisper.

There was no answer. It was dark in the hut, and cold. I felt my way to the stove, feeling sure there'd be matches, and there were, in the last place I looked (a biscuit tin with a lid). I struck one, searched around for a lamp, burnt my fingers then struck another, hoping they weren't in short supply and making a mental note to add matches to my shopping list for next time. I didn't see a lamp at first, but a torch hung beside the stove on a hook. I climbed up on the stool and flipped its string handle free.

Moving tiny pools of light around the hut, I felt like a criminal. Guilty and excited.

There were storm lamps at both windows, another balanced by the stove and a fourth by the stairs. I lit all four to dispel the awful loneliness of the place. And to warn Finn. I didn't want to leap out at him like a burglar when he arrived.

Replacing the matches, I tripped, knocked over a chair and heard a crash. But instead of a pool of wet among the pieces of broken china, I found a thin disk of frozen tea.

Minutes passed. I sat on the little bench next to the lamp and rubbed my hands together, shivering and wishing I could build up the fire. But this was his home not mine. And I wasn't much good at building fires in any case.

The wind had picked up. Booming waves crashed against the banks of pebble. The hut was cold and full of ghosts; I couldn't think what I was doing here or where Finn could be. Perhaps he had other friends. This had never occurred to me. There wasn't room in my fantasy of our relationship for others.

I stamped my feet and jumped up and down to get warm. Then I pulled one of the striped blankets off the bench, wrapped it round my shoulders and huddled on the bench in the alcove, increasingly drowsy, shivering, listening to the sea and waiting for Finn.

The click of the latch woke me instantly.

Finn stared. 'What are you doing here?'

Too many words choked up in my throat, and I reached for my satchel, fingers stiff with cold. 'I've brought some things.'

But he had already turned away and my heart sank. I had imagined a confident dropping by, a reunion of equals. I had imagined the sun low in the sky and the beach pink and gold as we chatted casually, easily, over black tea. But this?

Finn arranged twigs, kindling and logs in the stove. He lit it and stood back for a moment as it smoked, then caught, crackled and began to roar. I watched his profile, wondering whether he was searching for the words to tell me to get out. And like a pathetic sap, I felt tears burning the back of my eyes.

Silent and cold and blinking with unnatural rapidity, I tried to think of something with which to break the silence.

Finn still had his back to me.

With trembling hands I unpacked my treasures. Lamb chops wrapped in bloody paper from the butcher. A loaf of granary bread. A box of Typhoo tea. A pint of milk. A jar of jam. A book, *Tales of the High Seas*, stolen from Barrett. Laying them out on the bench, I suddenly wished I'd brought more exotic offerings: cashmere blankets and soft woollen socks, rare volumes of English history, a ship in a bottle. Gold, frankincense, myrrh.

But Finn was staring at me now. 'I don't know why you've come.'

My heart stopped. I want . . . I want to . . . I want you . . .

I fled. In my damp clothes, in the night, with the tide racing in and my eyes flooded with salt, I ran. All the way back to my real home, the only place I belonged.

'Hey, look who's here!' Gibbon, hunched over a history essay in our study, was delighted at this turn of events. He had obviously resigned himself to a slow night. 'Back from servicing granddad?'

Across the room, Reese said nothing. His position in the hierarchy was delicate. Barrett sat at the fireplace, charring bread on a fork. A small heap of stolen coal flickered blue with flame but did nothing to warm the room.

'Come on, loverboy, show us your stuff.' Gibbon giggled at the brilliance of his own repartee.

Barrett pulled his fork out of the fire and waved it at me encouragingly. 'Go on then.' He made obscene sucking noises, leading the way.

I looked from one colossal cretin to the other, then placed my hands on Gibbon's desk and leant right into his face, lips puckered for a kiss.

He drew back sharply and I slid my foot under the front leg of his chair, flicking it upwards. The crash and howl that followed distracted Barrett long enough for me to stroll from the desk to the fire and drop Gibbon's essay on to the coals. The cheap paper smouldered for all of three seconds before bursting into flame.

Reese's hand flew to his mouth, hiding an expression of delight.

I walked past the wailing Gibbon (despite the impressive gash at the back of his head, he managed a respectable lunge) and closed the study door in his face. The torrent of abuse that followed is not worth repeating.

Gibbon spent the night in the sanatorium while I tried to anticipate his next move. It was much easier to get inside his brain than Finn's, despite the fact that his psychopathic tendencies took me to places I'd rather not go. A few days later when the smell of rotten fish began accompanying me to lessons, I almost had to admire him, though the idea stank (literally) of Barrett's more subtle intelligence. By preference, Gibbon would have dropped an anvil on my head.

Suddenly there were kippers everywhere. In my bed, my shoes, my cap, my blazer, book bag, PE kit. It was a hellishly effective plot, a smell impossible to remove by methods available to a schoolboy, and by the time our housemaster cottoned on to foul play, I had acquired a new name and a reputation for putridness.

Ferreting kippers out of my personal belongings took up most of my spare time for the better part of a week. But I knew better than to complain or acknowledge the offence, and eventually the hostilities faded. Throughout this period, Reese provided solace in the form of the occasional small smile or furtive greeting, for which I actually felt grateful. And when I took to wandering off behind the playing fields and into the woods, he often followed a few paces behind like a dutiful Indian wife. An old yew hedge, nearly hollow on the inside, provided an excellent sheltered place to sit and read. It was damp, but so was everywhere else. I had moments of being almost happy there, and only occasionally gave in to the misery of so much lost, so much nearly won.

8

I didn't need Finn.

So the next time we ran down to the causeway, an afternoon in mid-November, with the trees bare and the days only a few hours long, I didn't slow down, didn't look left or right, didn't acknowledge that anyone (much less anyone I knew) lived in the little hut. And yet . . . physiology had its own imperative, and there was no point pretending that my racing pulse and flushed face had everything to do with exertion.

Reese panted along at my side. He hung around in my vicinity with such persistence these days that we were halfway to becoming a comedy act – Kipper and Reese, the two stooges – and I tolerated his presence because it made me look less friendless. When we rounded the rat's nose, I slowed, and stopped. Reese hesitated, but after a moment glancing hesitantly from me to the disappearing pack, he ran on.

Such a courageous boy I was. To act brazenly under such scrutiny *and* risk further injury to my wounded heart. Ah, the resilience, the blind, dumb persistence of youth.

There was smoke coming from the chimney. Driven by anger and a degree of fatalism, I opened the door without knocking. I'm back, I said silently, boldly. Take it or leave it.

And here's the miracle. Finn's expression (unless I have rewritten history, unless I was unable to read it at the time, unless wishing has the capacity to pervert truth), his expression was not shocked, *but relieved*.

'Hello,' I said, my mouth curled into a little satirical grimace, my spirit cautiously elated.

He actually smiled. At my foolish runner's kit, perhaps, or my brazen expression, my vulnerable legs. At my idiot's audacity. My barefaced cheek. I didn't care why.

He smiled.

Then he took a saucepan down from above the stove and left the hut. When he returned, it was sloshing with water and smelled of brine. Placing it on the iron stove he dumped in half a dozen potatoes, scooped some lard into a heavy frying pan and waited for it to melt. With infinite care, he placed a flat brown fish in the sizzling fat and as it cooked, put two plates on the wooden table beside the stove, pulled two forks and two knives out of a drawer in the table, and turned to me. Paused. Spoke softly.

'I'm no good at company.'

Did the words carry a hint of explanation? Not that it mattered. I'd already forgiven him.

'Sit,' he said.

I sat. No more good at being company than he was at having it.

And suddenly I was starving. Starving despite the silence,

the absence of the sweaty wool and foot smell of ninety other boys. I forced myself to eat slowly, not to bolt my food like a dog in case someone arrived mid-bite to take it away. I still finished before him.

Finn made tea and we sipped it and listened to the sea while this thing I didn't dare name glowed between us. And then all of a sudden I couldn't stand the silence so I began to tell him about my family, and my first two schools, and Reese and Barrett and Gibbon, and whatever else popped into my head.

He listened politely, without comment, head turned slightly away from the sound of my voice. There were none of the usual listening comments you expect from normal people, or the hilarious cracks I might have received from my schoolmates. Instead he just sat, face composed, dark hair hiding his expression – if he had one. He might have been asleep for all I knew, so complete was his lack of response. And yet, I thought I could *feel* him listening, I could almost see my words wandering in long trails around his head, circling, searching, until he sighed and yielded and granted them entry. My face flamed with the joy and the shame of exposure, while Finn sat silent and safe behind his fringe of hair, behind the long black lashes that guarded his eyes and his thoughts and the entrance to his soul.

After a while I ran out of words and fell silent, stubbornly awaiting a response. Perhaps no one had ever explained the concept of a conversation to him. As the minutes ticked by and he said nothing, I felt an irresistible urge to laugh, conceding game set and match to his talent for silence. I gave up and asked how he'd ended up living here.

He appeared not to have heard the question, but just as I was about to repeat it, he started speaking, slowly, feeling his way step by step in case the words contained a trap. 'The hut belonged to my gran.' He paused. 'She taught me history and reading. And how to handle a boat. I cooked for her because her eyes weren't much good towards the end.'

This sudden disclosure caught me entirely off guard and I scrabbled in my brain for an appropriate comeback, anything to keep him going. *Her name, what she looked like, how she ended up living in a half-ruined hut on the beach?*

'She grew up in Ipswich.' He turned to me, head tilted slightly. 'In a big house in town. She wanted to be a teacher, but her father didn't believe in educating girls. She eloped at eighteen and he left everything to her brothers when he died.' Finn paused and looked at me gravely. 'Though he might have done that in any case.'

I concentrated hard, trying to produce a clear picture from these fragments of family tree.

'She moved to the hut when her husband died. Other people lived here then – fishermen, families.' He paused. 'People were poor then. It didn't cost much.'

I searched the shadows of his face for marks of his past. Surely the preceding generations had crept into the colour of his eyes, the curve of his brow, the shape of his cheekbones. I wondered if his ancestors had survived to the present day in a way mine hadn't. Our family photographs showed respectable bankers and lawyers in sober Edwardian clothes. They stared at the camera, expressionless, and never seemed related to anyone in particular. Neither of my parents would have been able to imbue the previous generations with life, in the unlikely event that they might try. My history had evaporated before I was born.

I sat motionless. When Finn finally looked up, remembering me, he yawned and indicated the bench. 'It's late. You can sleep there. The privy's out back, I'll show you.'

The tide would be high. There was no way I could get back to school. Terror and resignation swept over me at once, and as I met Finn's steady gaze – a little puzzled, a little impatient – I realized the decision had somehow been made. Heart pounding, I followed him out to the old-fashioned camp toilet. OK, I thought, I'll think about it tomorrow. I'll get away with it somehow. I'll . . .

The wind whipped the heat from my clothes, the reason from my brain. Gazing up at the sky, I sought the two constellations I knew, as if somehow I could spin an astronomy lesson from so vast a transgression.

When I returned, there was a lumpy pillow on the bench and a pile of blankets – the thick striped ones, faded with age. I didn't want him to go yet.

'Your gran . . . when did she die?'

'Four years ago. The solicitors located her youngest brother. He came up from Cornwall to pay for the funeral. They hadn't spoken in years.'

'Didn't anyone ask what would happen to you?'

'I told him I'd arranged to live with my mother. He didn't check.'

More holes in the net. I tried to imagine fending for myself at – at what? Twelve?

'But didn't your mum . . .'

He waited.

'Didn't she . . . does she know you live here?'

His expression was mild. 'She was sixteen when she had me, nineteen when she left.' Finn leant down and picked up the little cat. 'I don't remember what she looks like.'

I thought of my own mother, reliable as the furniture.

There was so much more to ask, but the conversation was over. A complex contract was in the process of being forged, whereby Finn agreed to tolerate my presence and I agreed to worship him – totally, but carefully, so as not to destroy the fragile equilibrium of his life.

The cat leapt from his arms and Finn crossed over to the kitchen to close the vent on the stove. Without saying goodnight, he handed me a lamp and disappeared up the stairs. I unfolded the blankets and crawled between them, lying for a long time wrapped up warm against the night, listening to the wind and looking at the pictures on the walls and the trembling shadows cast by the little flame.

I can be there again now, huddled in a private pocket of warmth as the fire dies and the hut cools, snug against the roar of wind and sea, wrapped in blankets permeated with Finn's smoky-wood smell, and always aware of the other presence in the loft above me, mysterious and powerful as an angel. After all these years, I can barely think back to that night without succumbing to emotions both wonderful and terrible, to a feeling as deep as the sea and as wide as the night sky. It was love, of course, though I didn't know it then, and Finn was both its subject and object. He accepted love instinctively, without responsibility or conditions, like a wild thing glimpsed through trees.

At last I extinguished the lamp, though according to my watch it was still early. And then, divided from the night by nothing more than four flimsy walls and an idea of a friend, I fell asleep.

9

Finn was gone by the time the sun woke me. I felt disconcerted by his ability to slip out without my hearing but there was no time to hang about. I dressed quickly, said a quick prayer of thanks for the low tide, and ran back to school, hoping to slip in to breakfast without anyone having noticed I was gone.

At the school gates, my housemaster stood waiting with the police.

My parents were phoned and informed that I was still alive, and a lifeboat search called off. I was punished for this extraordinary infringement of school rules by being placed under house arrest and losing all privileges. In a serious talk with my housemaster, I was threatened with expulsion, which for once bothered me.

And yet, oddly, no one asked where I'd been when I failed to return to my room all night, or what I'd done. This I found puzzling, satisfying and hilarious, as if 'off school grounds' were a generic place that didn't require further specification. This omission confirmed my faith in the imbecility of the so-called *real* world, the one in which I pretended to live most of the time. I ignored the glares of authority and the taunts of my room-mates, but most of all I ignored Reese, who lurked and lingered and buzzed round my head with his sticky friendship and his sly questions and the barest suggestion that *he knew*.

Knew what, I wondered. Enough to tell?

I was kept under lock and key for nearly a month, until our break-up for Christmas, allowed only to shuffle to and from meals and lessons. There was nothing to differentiate the days. I wouldn't have minded so much if there'd been a way to tell Finn why I stayed away. Maybe he didn't care, but I often sat gazing out of the window like a sea captain's wife.

At the end of term, my father picked me up from school, shaking his head.

'I don't have to tell you how disappointed I am,' he told me. 'Not only are your grades appalling, but this other business . . .' He looked at me with an expression that was almost contempt. 'What were you thinking? What if you'd died of exposure, been hit by a car? How would we all feel then?'

How *would* we all feel, I wondered. I thought I knew how I'd feel. Dead and cold and stiff, my entrails twisted and septic in my decomposing body. Perhaps it would be a relief. I couldn't muster up the emotion to mourn this imagined loss of myself, nor could I shake the suspicion that I'd be better off without a body, or at least without this particular body. For one thing, there would be far less opportunity for random betrayal. No more awkwardness, no more fumbles, no more strained lungs and blotchy cheeks. I felt infinitely cheered by this possibility of losing my physical self.

'. . . your mother and I have had a long talk about the suitability of your continuing tenure at St Oswald's –'

'*What?*' I tuned back in to the conversation with a start. 'But I can't leave!'

My father looked at me, his expression puzzled and slightly disgusted. 'Just come along,' he said. 'We'll discuss it later.'

It was late afternoon when we set off, and most of the drive took place in the dark. After the first few miles I turned my brain to neutral and stared out into the black night, counting the headlights that cast long bright shadows up my window. Mile after mile, I thought about the only thing capable of occupying my thoughts.

Despite the late hour, my mother met us at the door with exclamations of welcome. She made cocoa, relieved me of my filthy clothes, and kissed me goodnight with nervy affection. There were neatly ironed pyjamas in my bottom drawer; I put them on and settled into the unfamiliar squishy comfort of home. Although I'd been away nearly four months, nothing in my room had changed. In fact, nothing much had changed since I began my life of indentured education twelve years ago. Except me, of course, but I barely counted.

The next morning I slipped back into my old skin like a seasoned panto actor slipping into a horse suit. I knew the drill here (the rules, the disguises, the proper responses) the same as everywhere else.

Mother seemed pleased to see me, despite my disgrace.

For the three weeks of Christmas break, she doted on me as much as she knew how, and when it came time to return to school, she and my father appeared stymied by my good cheer. Perhaps I was settling in after all.

10

In company with the monarchy and the army, boarding schools of the 1960s comprised the last outposts of the poor shrunken British Empire – complete with a full set of nineteenth-century values. This meant we were ruled by a code of conduct that tolerated all flaws save those pertaining to loyalty and rank. Having violated neither, I was clasped on the shoulder and forgiven my previous term's crimes.

'Our relationships here are based on trust,' Clifton-Mogg intoned. 'We have been entrusted to educate you, and we trust you to behave with maturity and dignity. This term you have a chance to begin anew, and we have no doubt that you will uphold our trust like a man.'

He sounded shifty, as if he didn't quite believe the words he was saying, knew that I knew he didn't believe them, and knew that *I* didn't believe them either. Nonetheless, I set my features to indicate sincerity and could tell that he appreciated it; it made both our roles flow more smoothly. I, of course, had no trouble looking sincerely pleased; I intended to use this whole mutual trust business to clear off at the first possible opportunity. Tides willing.

Tides were crucial. The journey from my dormitory to

Finn's hut took thirty-five minutes (twenty minutes along the footpath to the edge of the causeway, fifteen minutes to cross and reach the end of The Stele). There were, however, all manner of contingencies to consider. The footpath was slower than the road, but safer from discovery. There was a general limit of two hours on either side of low tide during which it was possible to cross from the island to the mainland (and vice versa) without getting soaked, though this varied according to the phases of the moon and the height of the tides. Add it all up, and I had four hours at the hut (maximum) plus seventy minutes travel time. Give or take a few seconds. Of course there was always the possibility of straddling two tides, crossing two hours after the low tide and returning two hours before the following low tide: twelve hours minus four hours plus travel equals nine hours ten minutes. Or staying all night and hoping for the best. But I wasn't keen to try that again in a hurry. At least not without a more sophisticated plan in place.

It may sound fanatical to time everything out so carefully, but minutes were what we lived by: stolen minutes, minutes between lessons, four minutes to smoke a fag, twenty minutes for a pint at the pub, free periods during which forged exam papers or contraband could be purchased. Every minute was crucial in the race from lesson to town shuttle bus, and from town to catch the last bus back (fifteen minutes) or be stuck hitchhiking (thirty-plus minutes), finding a taxi (up to an hour and a near-insane extravagance), or sprinting the four miles back from town (twenty-six to forty minutes, depending on fitness).

And so, tide chart tucked neatly into my book of Latin verbs, I made the necessary calculations and planned my next campaign.

This time I bought bacon and teacakes, two cans of baked beans, twelve sausages, a jar of Colman's mustard, and matches. A schoolboy's idea of necessities. In addition, I had a copy of *Moby Dick* and a fairly new edition of the latest James Bond (much in demand) stolen from the school library. From what I could tell, Finn read a good deal, and appeared to have memorized the hut's meagre collection in its entirety; his appetite for fiction was considerably stronger than mine. I suppose there wasn't much else in the way of entertainment by the sea. And I, after all, had him.

In my impatience, I arrived at the beach an hour early on the first Saturday morning of the January term. The outgoing tide still covered the causeway in a foot of frigid green water, but I was unwilling to hang about in the cold. Removing shoes and socks and rolling up my trousers, I plunged in, finding myself first ankle-deep, then knee-deep, and then, panicking, thigh-deep in icy water and mud, overstuffed satchel balanced on my head, unable (and unwilling) to turn back. I lost all feeling in my feet almost immediately, which rendered me even more clumsy than usual. My arms ached with the weight of the heavy bag.

About halfway across I realized what an idiot I was. The current was so strong that I could easily be swept out to sea and drowned. When I stepped on something that rocked, and slipped sideways, terrifying seconds passed before I regained my balance. By now the food and I were soaked.

This is how people die, I thought, intrigued despite my predicament. This is how people get swept away and make next day's newspaper headlines (*Schoolboy Drowns, World Indifferent*) with no mention of what the aforementioned schoolboy was doing standing in the middle of a treacherous tidal canal with a bag on his head to begin with. I tried to brace myself, pausing to get my breath back as I imagined the private glee that would greet so tragic an announcement. I would be written off once and for all as the colossal imbecile the school had always suspected. Although it would require a certain amount of speaking-ill-of-the-dead, I would be eulogized as an incompetent, sexually suspect cretin. And for once they'd be right, I thought, choking as I inhaled a lungful of wave and sank to one knee, eyes clenched against the dark face of the sea.

With a final Herculean effort, I threw myself exhausted on to the sandbank and looked over at the line of huts. No sign of Finn, thank God. Even the thought of the *possibility* of his presence made me tremble.

It was nearly twenty minutes before I managed to wring the salt water from my clothes as best I could, gather my belongings, and set off again. I arrived cold and wet, teeth chattering, and tapped on the door. Finn answered immediately, seemingly unsurprised at – or by – my appearance. He raised an eyebrow, but offered no reproof.

'Come in,' he said, with an expression that was neither sympathetic nor amused, but contained minute traces of both. 'You haven't really got the hang of this, have you?'

11

'The high-water mark is advancing quickly,' he told me, eyes politely averted as I changed out of my wet school uniform and into a woollen sweater (his), and a threadbare towel. 'Geologically speaking, that is. The high tide only began cutting us off in the last decade.'

Peering out of the hut's window I could see the sea, only about fifty feet away. It wasn't much of a distance, particularly considering that the tide was now at its lowest.

Finn followed my gaze. 'If you compare the coastline to maps from a hundred years ago, you can see how much it's changed.'

I tried to dry my legs without giving away too much of my physique. Not that it mattered; Finn never seemed to notice me the way I noticed him. If I'd affected an eyepatch, dyed my hair purple, and developed a lisp he wouldn't have blinked.

'We never used sandbags until recently. Last year storms flooded the house for three weeks, I lived upstairs and wore waders to light the stove. It wasn't much fun.' He reached over me for a book, a collection of local maps.

'Look,' he said, placing it on the table and opening to our part of the east coast. 'These lines show the shape of the coast in 1800, 1850 and 1900.' I followed his finger as it swept down the page.

'Who owns the land?'

'It's common land, owned by the town since 1656. The island was still attached then.' He pronounced words quaintly, with his gran's old-fashioned accent. She had taught him to read, taught him the history of the area as she'd learnt it.

I studied the map, still thinking about the hut, flooded all those weeks in the icy winter months. The thought made me shudder.

'What if something happened?' I asked, tucking the towel round my waist, and not adding 'to you'. 'In a storm or something.'

Finn shrugged but I knew the answer. He had no one. In a panic of pride, responsibility and self-importance, I thought, *I will be the one to care.* I will take over the role of guardian, family, friend, all.

'There was once a city nearby, quite a big city, between AD 600 and 1200. I sometimes find bits of it on the beach.' He crossed to the window sill. 'Look.'

I looked. In his hand lay a smooth piece of pottery and a coin. He held them out to me and I took them, turning them over carefully. I knew about the city; it was part of the legend of St Oswald's, famous mainly for the nineteen churches drowned with the rest of the town in a great medieval storm.

The pottery looked like every other uninteresting bit of

terracotta I'd ever seen, but the coin was beautiful despite its corroded faces – dark grey with the remnants of a man's head on one side, a sun on the other. I wondered who the man was, and how long ago he had lived.

Finn looked at me, as if considering the quality of my thoughts, then stood up to signal an end to today's line of enquiry. The cat stretched and twined itself around his legs in easy ownership before returning to its place by the fire.

Oh, that I were the cat upon that hearth!

I followed Finn outside and together we combed the width of the beach, picking up wood and pieces of black beach coal for the fire. Despite it being the height of winter, the day had turned out sunny, clear and bright, and I began to sing, choppily, everything in my extremely limited back catalogue of tunes. I started with 'All Things Bright and Beautiful', and was well into quite a moving rendition of 'It's Now or Never' in my best Elvis Presley croon before Finn grimaced and threw the biggest stone he could find in my direction.

There was plenty of driftwood at the tidemark, most of it waterlogged. The sea was rough, and the sun managed to raise the air temperature well above freezing, but after ten minutes my fingers were stiff and blue. Finn gazed at the water.

'I've got to check my traps,' he said, without looking at me. 'You can't swim, by any chance?'

Of course I could swim, having had swimming lessons force-fed at every grim institution I'd attended since birth. It was yet another facet of the empire mentality, part of our preparation for survival on the *Cutty Sark*, HMS *Victory*, *The Titanic*. I looked out at the grey sea uneasily. On the other hand, I wasn't anxious to show off my skills here (on the North Sea) and now (January). One submersion a day was more than enough.

'I'll wait here,' I said, trying to sound casual, as Finn dragged a long green kayak down from behind the house and slid it into the sea. The cat followed, and he clicked his tongue at it, but at the last moment it turned away.

Then, without a pause, he was off, slipping into the boat like a gymnast, one hand on either side of the cockpit, settling quickly, and in the same movement beginning to paddle; left-right-left, smooth and expert. I didn't understand how he remained steady in such a fragile-looking craft, but he and the boat cut through the water with easy grace, as if the sea were a pond on a still day in June. He was nearly out of sight behind the swells when I saw the tiny craft swerve neatly to face the shore, and there he was, gripping a red buoy in one hand. I watched as he hauled the trap up, transferred its contents to a deep canvas bag, and then paddled to the next. Now that I knew what to look for, I could see the buoys, five of them, strung out in a line parallel to the coast.

For as long as I could stand it, which wasn't very long, I waited on the beach. Then retreated to watch from the window. It required long minutes and a great deal of pain for my fingers to thaw from grey back to pink.

When Finn returned, I could almost feel the heat radiating off him, and his hair was slicked back with seawater and sweat. In one hand, he held the lumpy canvas bag drawn tight at the top with rope. I stared at it. Whatever was in it was alive. He laughed at the expression on my face and dumped the bag behind the hut, returning to the edge of the sea to fill a large bucket with water. Without waiting for instruction, I ran after him (shivering after the warmth of the stove) to haul the kayak up to the house. He accepted my help without comment.

'Do you like crabs?' he asked as he dumped at least two dozen of the large brownish creatures into the bucket.

I didn't know whether I liked crabs. I couldn't remember ever having eaten one and based on the look of the things felt quite sick at the prospect. Finn kept two back, placed a board on top of the bucket, and stood for a moment awaiting my answer.

'I think so,' I said nervously, and he nodded approval. And so I watched, transfixed, as he threw onions and bacon into the bottom of a saucepan.

My safe, conventional suburban upbringing had involved the consumption of food, but preparation had always been the sole domain of adults. I could open a fridge or a biscuit tin, hack a wedge off a piece of cheese or cut a slice of bread. But I couldn't make a meal out of something I pulled from the sea. It had never occurred to me that food could be found somewhere other than on the high street. In my family it came from my mother, who fetched it home in bags and cans and neatly wrapped packages from the butcher's.

Finn prepared the crabs. It wasn't nice to watch, but I forced myself not to be squeamish, following my own rules as I invented them.

Rule number four: Don't look away.

Gripping the first live crab in one hand, he plunged a small sharp knife through its mouth and up between its eyes. Next he pushed it into the crab's underside, cut along the centre line, ripped off the top shell, dug the squashy brown lungs out and tossed them outside to the seagulls. He twisted the claws off, smashed them with a hammer and then tossed the broken creature and its parts into the smoking frying pan. It seemed cruel to me, and I hated it, hated him for what he was doing. But it didn't stop me admiring him as much as ever or perhaps more, despite what I naively took to be this streak of cruelty. It was only a crab, after all.

And I ate it, didn't I? And wasn't it delicious?

Finn offered tiny morsels of organs and flesh a piece at a time to the cat, who accepted each one delicately and swallowed without chewing. When it had eaten enough, it waved its tail, turned up its nose and walked away.

In January the evenings came early. We had to light the lamps before we ate. By then, the last glow of sunset had gone, leaving behind an almost full moon that reflected brightly off the sea, casting sharp daylight shadows. I told Finn I had to go and reluctantly changed back into my clammy school clothes. He walked with me as far as the causeway, pointing to the easiest crossing place.

'Will I –' halfway through the question I hesitated – 'see you soon?'

There was the longest pause, and I strained to interpret the silence. Was I trustworthy? Was my company more appealing to him than his own solitude? Was our version of friendship worth the trouble, the inconvenience?

And then came the smile, accompanied by a little mock-bow with one hand folded behind his back.

He's laughing at me, I thought. But my heart skittered with joy.

I crossed the sandbar without incident, not looking back, though I wanted to. And when I'd passed through the magic boundary on to the beach, back through the rabbit hole into my own world, I broke into a run. Without his presence to blind me, it suddenly mattered that I might be in trouble again.

This time I was lucky. Crossing the main courtyard, a group of boys returning from choir practice made so much noise in the dark that I easily slipped in behind them without anyone noticing. I pretended to sign in and by ten thirty I was in bed, staring blankly at a Latin translation that was due the following day.

'Hey, Barrett.' I called my neighbour softly. He threw himself over the edge of the partition between our beds, staring at me blandly.

I stared back. 'Have you done your translations?'

'Yes,' he said. 'But I'm not donating my hard work to the Save-the-Wanker Foundation.'

'I'll change it. Get some of it wrong.'

He considered this. 'What have you got?'

I'd spent most of my money on Finn. I thought for a minute. 'Fags?'

'Got some.'

'Magazines?' I had some old pornography from a previous transaction, third hand, somewhat soiled.

He snorted. Having seen them at least as often as I had, they'd lost a good deal of their power to excite.

'What then?'

'Two quid.'

'*Two quid?*' I was outraged. The sum was absurd, though I didn't have it in any case. 'Sod off, I'll do it myself.'

'Suits me.' He disappeared again, and after the usual jiggling, all fell quiet.

With a sigh, I went to work on Virgil. *Arma virumque cano*: I sing of arms and the man. Sleep was miles away and it felt good to think about something else.

Fifteen lines later, I shut off my light and used the darkness to dream about the sea beating against a different shore, two thousand years and a thousand miles away.

12

Everything I know about Finn came in fragments, tiny shards to number and label and fit together with fake-casual persistence. Did he notice how I scratched at the surface of his hut with my delicate tools? How I studied his life and times? He was the cat that walked by himself and all places were the same to him, but wasn't he also human? Was anyone immune to the sort of attention I offered?

The story circulating to explain my absences from school claimed that I periodically visited a desperate lecherous old townie for whom I was doling out personal services at a pound a shot. Sometimes it was a man, sometimes a desperate housewife, sometimes an ageing slapper with a yen for young boys.

Of course the official line on my whereabouts was slightly different: I told Clifton-Mogg I liked to commune with nature, an excuse he accepted with bored approval. It was a novel experience to find myself clinging to St Oswald's, terrified I might be found unworthy of the effort required to sustain me in their midst.

Not that I was willing to forego the risk that made the experience worthwhile.

I planned my next journey for a Saturday, when I might catch the end of the low tide after morning lessons. The return crossing wouldn't be possible until late night, but I was willing to swim back if I had to.

'Where you off to?' It was Reese.

'Nowhere.'

'Can I come?' Wheedling.

'Come nowhere?'

'You go to the beach. I know you do.'

I snorted. 'In January?'

His voice turned menacing. 'I know where you go. I've followed you.'

Jesus.

'You don't have to worry. I won't tell.'

'Tell what, exactly?'

'About your friend.'

'You're my only friend, Reese.' The attempt at sarcasm came out wrong, more sincere than I'd intended, and to my horror he blushed with pleasure. I looked up at him slowly, adjusting my gaze to a fine beam of intensity and lowering my voice to a whisper. 'And if you don't keep your mouth shut I'll have to kill you.'

His voice shook. 'OK.'

'Not that I'm hiding anything.'

'N-no.'

I felt a sudden twinge of compassion. 'Look. I'll take you with me sometime, I swear.' And then, unable to bear another second, I ran.

For once the crossing was easy, and I found Finn balanced on the hut roof, attempting to hammer down pieces of black asbestos tile where it leaked. He barely acknowledged my presence, which pleased me – I wanted to be taken for granted, considered part of his landscape. I slouched down on the south side of the hut, shielded from the wind, and began handing up tools as he needed them. The sun shone, he seemed content with my company, and an easiness settled over us. When I'd succeeded in passing every tool he owned up to the roof, I stretched out on the scrubby ground and closed my eyes.

'This is the life.' Based on unseasonable temperatures, the Met Office was predicting an early spring. Not that I put faith in weathermen, but the winter sunshine made me optimistic. I lay perfectly still, face pointed at the sky, and could actually feel my greyish pallor warming to gold. 'What's the worst thing about living by yourself?'

Finn looked at me over the edge of the roof, frowning. 'Sorry?'

'Oh, come on,' I said, venturing beyond my usual deference. 'There must be something. I know the *good* things. What about the rest? No one to talk to? Cooking for yourself? No post?'

He blinked, uncomprehending, and turned back to his work. 'Don't be daft.'

I propped myself up on one elbow and drew shapes in the sand. Well, it hadn't exactly been the scintillating conversation that attracted me in the first place. Finn seemed genuinely unclear as to the purpose of conversation. He could convey information. He could make an enquiry regarding something concrete or the advisability of immediate action.

69

But I knew if I asked which he preferred, cabbage or sprouts, or how he envisaged his future, or if he missed his gran, he would have no answer to give. Not because he was hiding the information, but because his mind didn't work that way. You might as well ask a duck what it thinks of capitalism.

I lay flat, considering these facts. The winter sun beat down, warming the bits of me that showed; the rest of me huddled further down into my overcoat.

It's not that he lacked poetry. But his poetry was of the body, not the mind. He spoke it in the way he moved, the way he held a hammer, rowed a boat, built a fire. I, on the other hand, was like a brain in a box, a beating heart in a coal scuttle.

'Don't you want to know the worst thing about school?' I held my breath, twitching the bait ever so gently across the surface of the pond.

There was a beat of silence. Then: 'All right.'

Well, well, well. I doubted he was interested in the answer, but he was making an effort. There was something hugely touching about the unnaturalness of it.

'The worst thing is . . . the lousy food, the cold, the boredom, the isolation. Winters that go on forever. Years stretching ahead, incarcerated behind brick walls with no hope of reprieve. The rules.'

Finn leant over to look at me, bemused.

I was on a roll. 'Not to mention the loneliness. And at the same time, the crowdedness. The never being really alone, just to think, or rest or do something private – anything private. You can't even go to the toilet in private. And if you want company, real company, not just people hanging about making a noise, that's when you realize how lonely you are.'

Finn had stopped working to listen. He was silent for a long moment, as if testing the words one by one to see if they made a connection, lit a light bulb, rang a bell. I watched the process, fascinated, watched the possibilities flit across the surface of his face. Hopeful, ever hopeful.

And then I watched him lose interest. The roof needed fixing. The tide was high. A few years ago he'd lived with his gran and now he lived alone. These were the facts. Conjecture of the sort I thrived on made no sense to him at all.

I wanted to say *Jesus, Finn*, didn't anyone ever talk to you? But I could imagine that no one had. People around here didn't waste words; language was a tool, not a treat. You didn't roll it around on your tongue, revel in it.

I sighed. And yet . . . how was it that Finn's silences turned my words to dust? No matter how heartfelt my thoughts, the noises I made when I was with him took on the quality of monkeys jabbering in trees. While his silence had the power to shatter glass.

I needed him to talk. 'What's your first memory?'

He blinked at the absurd intimacy of the question and for a moment remained silent. But just as I moved on to something else in my head, he answered. 'I remember my mother, talking. Shouting, actually, before she left.' He paused again. 'I was nearly three.'

I guessed that his mum ran away because she was too young and too selfish to look after a baby. Or that rural life seemed unbearably dull to a beautiful nineteen-year-old. You only had to look at Finn to know she couldn't have been plain. Poor girl. Poor Finn.

He caught my expression, and smiled. 'You needn't look so tragic. You don't miss what you haven't got.'

I nodded, composing my features into a man-of-the-world's appreciation of emotional complexity. It was something I understood, but not exactly in the form that he presented it. In my conventional middle-class world, mothers loved their children and fathers pushed them away for their own good. I was ready (anxious even) to have these truths dispelled, but it took some consideration.

Finn climbed down, cleaned each tool carefully, and replaced them in the wooden toolbox he kept under the stairs. Then, without a word, he set off, wading through the channel, which had started to fill. I followed, reluctantly, wondering if I could run back and get the kayak.

'The earliest thing I remember is the sea,' he said, heading north along the beach and tossing a stone far out into the surf. 'Gran used to put me out on a blanket on the beach when I was a few weeks old and let me entertain myself watching the gulls. I still remember the smell of that blanket.' He paused, nose in the air, as if he might still catch a whiff of salt and old wool. 'Later I sucked pebbles. Mum said I'd choke on them and die.'

There was nothing of self-pity in this observation.

'One day, I got tired of lying still and just stood up and started to walk. Sometimes people on the beach brought me home when I wandered too far. Other times Gran had to walk the dykes calling my name. She always worried that I'd drown.' He gazed up at the gulls, standing very still.

While he spoke, I collected skipping stones. I positioned myself carefully, put a perfect flick and spin on my best flat stone and watched it sail into the sea at exactly the right angle, spinning backwards as it hit and leaping up again immediately, then bouncing again and again and again until it had skipped sixteen times. Glancing back, ready to accept Finn's admiration with appropriate modesty, I saw that he was still watching the gulls and hadn't noticed.

'I would set off, always in the same direction with the sun behind me. No child walks into the sun,' he said, turning to me, as if worried about my future. 'Remember that if you ever lose one.'

We had come to another channel further up the beach, where the river met the sea in a ferocious rush. Finn pulled off his jersey and walked in without pausing, his shirt soaked and snaking around his narrow waist and hips. It was quite deep in the middle and required him to swim backstroke with one hand in the air to keep the jersey dry. I dipped my foot in cautiously and jerked it out immediately. The cold was obscene. My heart sank as I watched Finn clambering out on the other side, his shirt and khaki trousers flapping in the icy wind. I never met anyone who felt the cold less.

I sighed. This time there was no way round it, I would have to undress, or risk ruining my school uniform. I left my coat on the beach, stepped slowly out of my trousers, unbuttoned my white shirt, stuffed my school tie into a pocket, removed my socks and shoes and rolled them up together into a clumsy bundle.

It was the thought of standing for any length of time on the bank – exposed and blue with cold in the underwear I'd been wearing for most of the week – that drove me to take the plunge sooner rather than later. Losing my balance almost immediately, I tried regaining it with Finn's backstroke trick, but instead slid entirely under the freezing water, clothes and all, swallowing a huge mouthful of water and earning a snort of derision from the bank.

Finn waded in and dragged me up on to the bank, shivering and dripping in my horrible white pants. I hated the feel of clammy underwear against my skin, knew I looked pathetic with my poor shrunken parts clearly outlined within, and that I would feel infinitely worse once I'd managed to drag my sodden trousers over shaking limbs. But despite the acute physical discomfort, the embarrassment proved more or less incidental. As usual, Finn seemed barely to have noticed my predicament. He was still talking, as if the awkward crossing hadn't registered on his radar at all.

'. . . there was a place I used to hide, up on the cliffs. A sort of cave. It was carved into the clay. You had to climb up from the beach to get to it.'

We were walking along the shingle again, but the chafing of salty wet clothing had begun to turn my thighs and the contents of my pants so raw that I managed less than half an hour before I had to sit down, furious, cold, and in pain – a kind of silent protest. After hovering a moment, Finn sat down next to me.

'Here, take this,' he said, pulling the thick jersey over his head.

This was no time for heroism and I didn't pause before accepting it. Pushing head and arms into the thick oily wool, surrounded by the woodsmoke smell of him and wrapped in the heat from his body, I felt almost dizzy with relief.

'Have you rested enough?' he asked eventually, uncharacteristically solicitous. 'We can go back if you like.'

Cheered by even so small a pledge of concern, I glanced down, silently telegraphing the plight of my genitals. In vain.

'Let's go then.' Before I could react, he had leapt to his feet and was off.

I sat upright. '*Go where?*' The words came out as a bleat. When there are only two of you and you are always the last to know what is happening, you develop an acute (and accurate) sense of misgiving.

Finn didn't answer, so I scrambled after him, chafing and puffing.

After another agonizing mile I noticed that the dunes had evolved into cliffs, and now rose steeply – thirty, forty, fifty feet up into the bright sky. Finn stopped, stepped back with his eyes shaded against the glare, scanned the surface of the cliff, turned, and without a word of warning began to climb.

I stood below, staring up after him. He climbed like a monkey, quick and agile, finding hand- and footholds where none existed. I didn't have a clue where he was headed; the sun's uniform glare erased all features from the surface of the cliff. But, ever the dutiful acolyte, I dug my toes into the soft chalk, pulled myself up, and followed the leader. Slowly.

It took every ounce of strength and concentration to cling to the surface of the cliff. My arms trembled violently with the effort, my toes slipped repeatedly off tiny crumbling ledges. The insides of my thighs were agony, my wounds scraped raw and anointed with salt.

I hate you, I thought, *I hate you* with your *bloody* nature-boy airs and your *bloody* forced-march voyage of *bloody* discovery.

I wondered then if Finn's personality worked on everyone, or whether I had just the right sort of mentality to fall in step with a self-centred hermit-boy crab-murderer.

The next time I looked up, Finn had disappeared.

I shouted his name but there was no reply. Fury drove me on, and fear. There was no easy way down from here, particularly as I couldn't see my feet, and didn't dare look at the beach in case of vertigo. I felt above for another handhold, grasped what felt like a solid clay ledge. But as I began to haul myself up one more time it crumbled into nothing, leaving me poised in mid-air like a cartoon coyote, clutching a handful of dust with an almost restful feeling of inevitability, with enough clarity and what seemed like enough time to save myself, but with nothing to stop me tumbling backwards and somersaulting over and over to smash and break and bleed to death alone and abandoned on the rocks below.

A hand shot out from nowhere and grabbed my wrist. The shock of it caused me to lose the rest of my fragile contact with the cliff and for a moment I dangled over the rocks below, scrabbling hopelessly for a foothold, rigid with terror, too terrified even to scream. And then a head followed the hand out above me, and a body leant out and another hand grabbed the waistband of my trousers, and half of me was scrambling and the other half being dragged thrashing up on to a ledge, which turned out to be a sort of a cave, the place Finn had been telling me about when I was barely listening due to the combined forces of pain and resentment.

It took a number of minutes for my heart to stop pounding and my breath to settle into something like a normal rhythm. Finn lay there, watching me and smiling as if he'd just told the funniest joke in the world.

'I am *not* bloody laughing.' My voice had gone hoarse with terror, my eyes swam with tears and I was furious: at his superior physical prowess, at my near-death experience, at the extent of my humiliation.

And then his expression became solemn and he looked at me gently, with genuine compassion. 'I'm sorry,' he said. 'I didn't mean to frighten you.'

Frighten me? Murder me, more like. I refused to answer, preferring to exert some miniscule power by remaining silent.

The entrance to the cave was narrow, but once I managed to wriggle into a more dignified position (flat on my stomach, arms folded under my chest, feet shoved deep into the recesses of the cliff) I realized I could stretch out with a fair degree of comfort. Physical comfort, that is. The prospect of having to climb back down kept me twitching with terror. And yet the sun beat down on the pale surface of the cliff with surprising warmth, we were out of the wind, and in the confined space Finn radiated heat and animal comfort beside me. I edged out, stretching over the terrifying drop and shifting forward until my left side settled into the graceful length of his body. In the tight space we fitted together like pieces of a puzzle.

Below us birds swooped and soared and I looked down on their backs as they flew, astonished, forgetting my fear. For that moment I was a god, with a god's eye view of the universe. Exhilarated, I moved to get a better look, inching further and further out, until Finn reached out a hand to pull me back. I hovered, held aloft by the strength and warmth of his grip, feeling the hot slow pulse of his fingers. I wanted to launch us both into the sky, to pull him up with me towards the sun where we'd fly like gods and never have to tumble back to earth.

He studied my face, amused by what he found there. The moment hovered, weightless.

I have often looked back at that moment and imagined history veering fractionally in one direction or another, imagined if I'd been a different person, or if he had, whether what followed would have been a different story altogether and the history of the world might have changed ever so slightly around us.

As it was, nothing happened except the two of us watching the sea come in and go out again, listening to the birds, sheltering from the rain when it came and lying silent as the sky changed from blue to white to gold. For hours we lay side by side, breathing softly together, watching thin rivulets of water run down the cliffs and into the sea, feeling the world slowly revolve around us as we leant into each other for warmth – and for something else, something I couldn't quite name, something glorious, frightening, and unforgettable.

For an instant I knew what it was to be immortal, to make the tides cease and time stand still.

And just this once, it wasn't Finn's power. It was mine.

Rule number five: Don't let go of the cliff.

13

According to Mr Barnes (history), the Dark Ages dawned in the middle of the fifth century with the decline of the Roman Empire. Roman occupiers had been settling in Britain all along – marrying, raising families, farming. But once Rome withdrew its central authority from Britain (AD 410), Saxon tribes invaded from Germany and divided England into four kingdoms: Mercia, Northumbria, Wessex, East Anglia. After a bloody and plague-ridden start, the Saxons settled down to a bloody and plague-ridden rule, until the Vikings came along to institute a new and improved (bloodier and more plague-ridden) kingdom.

Romance aside, no one with half a brain could be nostalgic for life in the Dark Ages. There were too many ways to live and die miserably in those days, particularly if you were a peasant. I could easily imagine myself as a peasant, dressed in scratchy homespun wool, trying to scrape a living from half an acre of land or maybe a single mangy cow. There would be a wife no one else wanted (pockmarked maybe, or lame) who'd probably die in childbirth leaving me no one to help with the cow or plough the little field. It would be cold all the time, and damp, and by midwinter we would run out of food and options while whatever children there might be wept with hunger, and later fell silent and died of starvation. I could easily picture the brutality and despair of this life, had no trouble imagining myself dying of something unromantic like plague, or something banal like a broken arm.

Mr Barnes was always keen to drive home the contrast between our charmed existence at St Oswald's and the brutal realities of history. Much to our delight, this included lurid tales of Viking torture and debauchery, our favourite being the blood eagle. The blood eagle required two deep vertical cuts to be made in a living man on either side of the backbone, severing the cartilage connecting ribs and vertebrae. Through these cuts, the live lungs were grasped and pulled backwards out of the chest cavity. The goal of this unimaginable act of brutality was to preserve the victim's life long enough to watch the lungs inflate outside the body like wings.

I thought of Finn's crab.

From what I actually managed to absorb in class (the experience was novel and even rather exciting), there emerged a fantastically romantic image of bloodthirsty armies clashing ferociously on barren plains, vast horned heroes sweeping from one end of the island to the other, 960 soldiers slain by a single warrior with a single sword in a single battle on a single day.

What more could a boy ask for? Especially a boy without the passion or the capacity to rip *any* creature's lungs out, even the lowliest.

You could almost hear the spark of genuine interest

ignite during lessons that term. Something about the anarchy and violence of the first millennium struck a chord in us where the hallowed achievements of ancient Egypt, Greece and Rome had failed. Which meant there was less groaning than usual when each of us was assigned an essay topic: Athelstan, The Venerable Bede, The Battle of Badon Hill, Alfred the Great, Offa's Dyke. St Oswald, patron saint of our beloved alma mater, fell to me. Gibbon had lobbied for Boudicca, which he saw mainly as an opportunity to look at drawings of naked breasts.

'Ho ho *ho*,' he leered, waggling pictures out of dusty history books as if they were *Playboy* centrefolds.

'Nice ones, Gibbon.' He'd been drooling over etchings of two-thousand-year-old breasts for most of the afternoon. I stretched, desperate to get out. 'Might go for a walk,' I muttered. Having checked the tides.

Reese jumped up. 'Can I come?'

Pulling on my coat, I avoided his eyes. 'No dirty pictures in nature.'

'You might get lucky, Kipper.' Gibbon, ever the optimist. 'Might see deer fucking.'

I ignored him. 'Come on then. It's going to be a lovely sunset.'

Gibbon erupted with laughter, prancing around the room cooing, 'A *lovely* sunset! A *lovely sunset!*' while Reese joined in nervously, not entirely sure whose side he was on. In the end, he chose the unambiguously heterosexual majority, as I knew he would. He had his own secrets, did Reese.

As I left the room, I could feel his eyes boring into the back of my head.

14

'So, what do you know about the Dark Ages?'

I'd been nervous. About returning to the hut, about seeing Finn. Even remembering our afternoon at the cave made me nervous. The longing to see him did not diminish with the passing days, nor did the feelings sort themselves into tidy strands of information in the way of geography or English grammar. None of what I felt could be explained by what I generally understood about sex. The ceaseless tangle of emotions confused me, forced me to wonder what I was. There was no one to ask.

But I couldn't stay away. And so, on a cold afternoon in early February I lay, one leg propped on the bookshelves at the bottom of my narrow bench, the other hanging over the side, asking about the Dark Ages while the fire in the stove crackled and Finn hunched over tiny scraps of feather, metallic foil from cigarette packets, and steel fish hooks, wrapping them securely with cotton to make lures. His cat glared and hissed at me whenever Finn wasn't looking, and when he chirped to it and stroked it absently, I could swear it sneered.

Finn answered after the usual pause. 'What do you know already?'

I told him my version of the first millennium and he snorted and shook his head in disbelief. 'How much does your education cost? You could save everyone a fortune by reading a book once in a while.'

I ignored him, reached out to the cat and received an ugly scratch for my pains. I took a swipe at the beast but it was already comfortably out of reach, grinning back over its shoulder.

'If you don't mind, I didn't exactly choose to be sent to the back of beyond to be bullied and buggered and starved.'

He appraised me. 'You don't look starved.'

I thought of the disgusting sausages filled with gristle and glue, the tasteless suet puddings, the stinking vats of boiled cabbage.

Finn walked over to the bookcase and pulled out an old-fashioned leather-bound book entitled *A Short History of Britain*. It smelled strongly of damp and must have had nine hundred pages. I groaned. 'Really. I don't need to know all that. Ten pages would be more than enough.'

'No, it wouldn't,' he said, dropping the huge book in my lap. 'You're amazingly ignorant. Especially with all your advantages.'

'Advantages?'

'A proper education is a privilege,' he said, a touch primly.

I laughed my best sardonic laugh and Finn looked at me sideways. 'You're actually quite proud of having failed so often, aren't you?' He turned away and behind his back I pulled a face.

This line of discourse infuriated me. For one thing, his imaginary version of school life bore no relation to reality, and he resolutely denied all my attempts to impart the truth. He imagined a world of frock coats and good manners, a respect for intellect and the individual, the mature exchange of ideas seasoned with healthy outdoor pursuits. I don't know how or where he came by this vision (it sounded like something out of ancient Greece to me), but he clung to it in the face of all evidence to the contrary, perhaps charmed by the idea of the social and economic gap between us. He was, after all, a boy who lived in a hut by the sea, while my parents holidayed in France and Spain, employed a cook and a part-time gardener, bought a new car every four years and had the means to purchase for their only son a dubious education that would (at the very least) guarantee entrance to adulthood with an ability to decline Latin verbs with a recognizably expensive accent.

Finn, in contrast, had nothing. Only a romantic past, floating present, and lack of future, any of which I would have sold my soul to possess.

With a sigh, I picked up the history book and began to read, of chaos and bloodshed, and gold coins bearing the heads of Kings Offa and Horsa, of cakes and ale and vast feasts of oxen and honey and geese.

I liked how wild they were and yet how domestic, the extreme possibilities of so much land changing hands with such frequency and violence, and in between, peaceful

farmers tending crops and carving fine sewing needles out
of bone.

'What about St Oswald?'

'What about him?' Finn came through, sat down very
close to me, took the book from my hands and began
flipping pages. 'There were two Oswalds, actually. Look:
"Archbishop of York – served at Ely Cathedral, tenth
century." The other was King of Northumbria, seventh
century. Boy warrior, on a mission to spread Christianity
and reunite the four kingdoms. He was hacked to death
in battle, torn limb from limb in Somerset.' He found what
he was looking for, a black-and-white photograph of the
head of a young man, a relief carving in stone. 'Here.
Oswald the King with his raven.'

I peered at it closely. The boy king was handsome,
beardless, dressed in flowing robes. The caption on the
picture read *Oswald of Northumbria,* AD *642.* I nodded,
struck by the features of the young king, by the strong
lines of the profile, the finely wrought mouth. In an instant
I knew for certain that the other Oswald, the archbishop,
did not – could not possibly – figure in my story.

I turned back to Finn, met his large dark eyes, and didn't
turn away. When he passed the book back to me his hand
was steady and the expression on his face unreadable.

'It's all in there.'

I looked at the book, then at Finn. In our dance of
friendship he led and I followed. At moments of intimacy
it was always he who pulled me close and I who drew
breath and trembled. It was always he who pulled away,
as well.

'I can't possibly read all this.'

He knew everything, of course he did. He knew all about both Oswalds and all about me. I wanted to beg him to drag one of the painted chairs in from the kitchen, to sit down and tell me everything he knew about history. I wanted to hear him speak softly, to say with fond contempt that I understood nothing, to protest that he'd have to start from the beginning, that it could take all night to make me understand. I wanted him to lean in towards me. I wanted to feel the warmth of his skin, breathe the warm salt smell of him.

'It'll take hours to get through.'

That infernal half-smile.

'Then you'd better get started,' he said, and left the room.

15

One of the last acts of the dying Roman Empire was to build a series of forts along the east coast of Britain to hold off the barbarian hordes. The forts, though mighty, didn't work as planned, and Germanic and Viking tribes soon overran the land.

The fort just up the coast from St Oswald's ended its life underwater in a great fourteenth-century storm during which an entire port and half a mile of coastal farmland disappeared under the sea, along with most of the town's inhabitants, its famous churches, and two hundred head of cattle. I had read in the local paper about unsuccessful attempts to explore the site. Underwater visibility in the area was always poor, and when it wasn't poor, it was abysmal. Even on the clearest day, a diver fitted with a lamp would be unable to read his own compass.

In Finn's history book, I found a footnote referring to an eighth-century monastery built within the walls of the fort, consecrated by Oswald the King. As I read, I experienced a genuine thrill as the scraps of history came together. Despite the fact that everything written so far had located him primarily in Northumberland near the borders of Scotland, here was written evidence locating Oswald on our coast. He must have travelled south to cement ties with the lower kingdoms of Wessex and East Anglia, establishing a monastery, and causing a huge heavy stone to be carved with a likeness and transported south from Holy Island to commemorate the event.

The face on the stele disturbed me. The boy king had been a great warrior, had died a hideous and dramatic death. He was larger than life, a gigantic presence from the past. But thirteen hundred years later he still looked like someone I knew, or would like to have known.

'Let's explore the fort.'

Finn sat opposite me, his brow furrowed with concentration as he wrapped his lure slowly and methodically with fine brown string. He didn't change expression and I wasn't sure he'd heard me.

When finally he looked up, he said, 'Can you empty the traps today?'

I sighed. The short answer was no, but honour required me to act. So I went to fetch the kayak. And in my thoroughly non-sectarian way, I prayed to whichever of the Oswalds happened to be listening.

Dear saint, dear saint, dear saint. Please St Oswald, let me manage this task. Please O Powerful One, deliver me from capsizing, from humiliation and death by drowning. If there is such a thing as a bloody buggering saint, be one and watch over me now. Amen.

If I'd been a better Christian I might have asked for a miracle. Instead, I gritted my teeth and half-carried, half-dragged the kayak down to the water's edge, stepped into it carefully and, legs extended, settled myself in the cockpit as I'd watched Finn do. My weight instantly displaced the few inches of water underneath us, beaching the boat firmly against sand and stones. Too late, I remembered the paddle and nearly flipped over in an attempt to retrieve it from the beach. I hoped Finn couldn't hear the horrible scraping noise the boat made as I jerked and shoved it out of the shallows.

Please God.

I hit the small choppy waves side-on – my next mistake – and took on water trying to nose out across them at a forty-five degree angle the way I'd seen Finn do. It was not gratifying to learn how much harder it was than it looked. I struggled to keep the boat steady, but my stability was compromised by sloshing and inadequate paddle rotation. I managed one good strong stroke on the left but inevitably followed up with a completely ineffective slice on the right.

Out of the corner of one eye I could see that Finn had descended to the edge of the water to watch my performance. By now I was drenched in sweat as well. If I capsized in this sea, I was finished. Drowning would be the best possible outcome, for my pride at least.

A few effective strokes managed to steady the little boat and I aimed for one of the buoys, steering as straight a path as possible but aware nonetheless of my zigzag wake. The waves rocked but didn't tip me over, and I remembered to twist the paddle with every stroke.

I can do this.

I could do it. I could, that is, until I got within two or

three feet of the red buoy, which floated above the trap. The current kept pushing me away so it took four different attempts at an approach before I managed to run over the damn thing, and in a death-defying turn based on Russian Cossack horseriders I'd seen in a newsreel, I reached under the kayak to grab the rope. Panting with exertion and fear, I laid the paddle flat in front of me across the deck, but instead of affording greater stability it slipped sideways with every swell, catching the little white crests of waves and flipping a bucket of seawater into my already half-submerged cockpit.

I was beginning to feel beleaguered.

Clinging to the buoy for dear life, I tried not to think of Finn (graceful and calm) as the sea spun me around and tried to wrench my arms from their sockets. Hand over hand, slowly, agonizingly, I hauled the rope up until the heavy wooden trap hung just below the surface. It teemed with crabs all piled together round the fish-head bait, groping and plucking at it with their heavy claws as I struggled to hang on to the canvas bag and trip the latch on the trap. Eventually, triumphantly, I did it – tipping a dozen of the lucky bastards back into the sea. Perhaps a giant crab would rise up on some future dark and stormy night and grant me three wishes.

The few that were left I picked up gingerly. They were too big to lift the way Finn had taught me with sand crabs, so I grabbed them wherever I could and screamed quietly when they latched, with surprising force, on to my fingers. Eventually I managed to shove a few into the sack, secure the opening, and kick the whole thing deep up under the bow. I didn't want it or its fiendish contents touching any part of my anatomy.

One down; four to go. The wind off the beach had picked up and I suddenly felt the futility of the exercise. Forget the rest of the traps. I'd be lucky to get myself, the boat, and my few thrashing passengers back alive.

And so I headed in, too tired to worry about the correct way to paddle a tiny boat in a dangerous sea; my every fibre straining to remain upright and alive. Finn shouted orders from the shore but eventually collapsed in mock-despair on the beach, head in his hands, unable to observe further calamity. The wind tried to prevent my approach, but the tide was coming in, and once I caught the waves, they carried me (gracelessly, side-on) towards the beach. Scraping bottom once more, I scrambled out, catching my foot under the seat to ensure the final humiliation: me, face down in three inches of water, and the kayak (specially built for stability and easy handling in rough waters) swamped. Finn looked simultaneously amused and appalled and I wondered if I were flattering his prowess by playing the clown. Surely I couldn't be this clumsy.

'Go and dry off,' he said, one eyebrow raised, and I trotted off in disgrace while he pulled the boat up on to the beach, tipped it on its side to let the water run out, and set it afloat once more.

Wrapped in a blanket (how many times had I found myself in this position?), I squinted through the window of the hut and watched from afar as he emptied and rebaited the remaining traps. He swung the kayak a hundred-and-eighty degrees with a quick dip of the paddle and if there was a wind and a current to drag and moan and toss him off course, he seemed oblivious.

So there he was, my boy-king, out and back in half an hour with a good haul of nearly three-dozen crabs. Most of them were destined for the local fish restaurant, where they would be boiled alive and pulled limb from limb by an unremarkable class of diners. We ate a whole crab each that night, the shells crushed and the bodies eviscerated by the warrior in all his cold-blooded splendour. The pinky-white meat we sucked out of each claw was sweet and oily and as fresh as the sea.

Back at school it was shepherd's pie: lumpy mash, tinned tomatoes and cheap mince swimming in orangey fat.

When we had finished eating, Finn wiped his face and hands on a tea towel and sat back as I collected my belongings in preparation for the trek back to school.

'I think,' he said, in the manner of a pronouncement, providing an answer to the question I had long ago forgotten asking, 'I think we should explore the fort.'

16

A group of students remained behind at St Oswald's during the break between Lent and summer terms to pursue areas of excellence (swimming, choir, chemistry) – although this was generally a cover-up for those boys whose parents lived abroad, or holidayed without them, or simply couldn't be bothered to have them at home. In the spirit of entrepreneurship, I forged a letter from Clifton-Mogg informing my parents that I would be staying at school during the break, and another to Clifton-Mogg from my parents with permission to return home by train. I had something of a talent for forgery and wondered if I'd found my calling at last.

The fortnight preceding the break was nerve-wracking, but I needn't have worried. Neither the school nor my parents noticed anything suspicious and I felt wonderfully smug at the successful planning of my enterprise.

'Parents not here yet, Kipper? Must have forgotten you,' Gibbon sneered. 'Wish I could stay and keep you company. But, bad luck. South of France again.'

'Father on the run from the revenue?' I didn't bother looking up.

He dropped a used condom on my textbook. 'A going-away present. Broke it in for you.' Across the room Barrett howled with mirth. 'At least you and Reese will have each other for company. You *have* had each other, haven't you?'

I sighed. Reese had been signed off to spend the holiday with an elderly aunt, but wouldn't be leaving till Monday. He was the perpetual fly in the perpetual ointment, was Reese.

So the last Friday of term, while most of the other students signed out to travel to Spain or Cornwall or France with their loving families, I packed my bag while Reese buzzed about.

'Where are you going?' He hovered, suspicious.

'Spain. I told you.'

'Where are your parents then?'

'I'm meeting them. Taking the train.' I continued to pack. He continued to hover.

'Could I meet your friend now? You promised.'

'I'm going away.'

'I'll follow you again.'

Again? That was it. I swung at him, catching him in the stomach. To my horror, he folded instantly and began to sob, and I felt tired and fed up and wished vaguely that I hadn't hit him.

'Oh, for Christ's sake, Reese.' I helped him up but he shook my hand off his arm with surprising violence. 'Look, I'm sorry I hit you. Stop crying for Christ's sake.'

I sat, embarrassed and unhappy, as he struggled to control his (embarrassed, unhappy) sobs. When at last his breathing calmed, I offered him water but he wouldn't take it, wouldn't speak, wouldn't even look at me, and so finally I picked up my bag and left. He just wasn't that important.

He realized this, naturally, with the perfect instinct a dog has for rejection. And just as naturally, he despised me for it almost as much as he despised himself.

I walked through the deserted school and caught the bus into town, where I'd arranged to meet Finn, but when I arrived at the market a few minutes early, he was nowhere to be seen. His menacing boss-lady fixed me with her beady eye and called me over.

'Your friend will be back in a minute.'

'I'll wait.'

For about ten minutes we sat in uncomfortable silence. At least I was uncomfortable; she looked as imperturbable as ever.

I got up and browsed the stalls but retraced my steps quickly, too excited by the prospect of the weeks ahead to miss out on Finn's return. He still wasn't there.

Boss-lady offered me a thoroughly unpleasant smile. I didn't want to know what she made of my presence here. It wouldn't have occurred to Finn to wonder.

'Must be boring for you hanging about. Has anyone ever looked at your future?' Her voice was slick as hair grease and I remembered the snake from *Jungle Book* even as I struggled to understand her meaning. Was she offering me a job in the civil service? But then it clicked and I recoiled in horror. Was it possible that she actually told fortunes?

I shook my head, no, embarrassed by this obvious ploy to extort money. Did I really need to be told I would meet a dark lady and settle down in a town beginning with 'S'? My future seemed too obvious to bother predicting. Finn's fortune would have been more interesting – I couldn't imagine how he would ever be anything but sixteen, anywhere but in that hut by the sea, his face and limbs any more or less graceful than they were now. It was like imagining a future for Peter Pan.

'Come with me.' She laid a hand like a pig's trotter on my shoulder and I searched frantically for Finn.

'Don't worry,' she said. 'There's time.'

The fact was, I didn't want to know. I didn't want to know that I was running out of life, that hard times lay ahead, that I was unlucky in love. I didn't want to know that all my money would be stolen from me by the one I loved most, that trust would turn out to be laced with deceit, that nothing was what it seemed, that my life would be riddled with bonuses disguised as catastrophes, or vice versa.

It was all too obvious in my case anyway.

'Never mind,' she said caressingly, 'we'll have a cup of tea while you wait.'

With no hope of escape, I followed her into the market cafe with its proud announcement of today's specials: pork chops and custard pie. I sat across from her at the table nearest the door while an ancient crone brought the tea.

'Let me look at you,' she said, when the thick white teacups had been placed on the table.

Although her face was squashy as a pudding, the eyes

set within it were glittering and hard. She fixed me with them and my heart stopped beating; it was only after some seconds that I remembered to keep breathing, and exhaled.

'There's a girl,' she said without preamble.

Of course there's a girl, I thought, performing the mental equivalent of eye rolling. Beautiful, like a princess, with a fat baby on each hip. I felt like laughing out loud.

She gave a little shrug of annoyance. '*Concentrate.*' It was not a request. She held up the little glass salt cellar from the table and I looked from her to it.

Oh, great, I'm about to be hypnotized and kidnapped now, sold into slavery as a . . . but exactly what would I be useful for? I stared at the salt cellar and once more nearly laughed when I thought about all the noise in my brain, and what she'd said, and it occurred to me that she was probably right, there were too many thoughts, too many sides to every object and every single person, too many attempts to make sense of it so that I always ended up confused and distracted and somehow out of control, whereas salt, a pillar of salt, like Lot's wife, or was it Orpheus, someone turned into a pillar of salt by looking back when he? – she? – wasn't supposed to. And while I was thinking all this, a picture came into my head, of a face, not altogether human, and rippled as if separated from me by a thick plate of glass. It was a girl and I knew her the way you know someone in a dream, a familiar packaging of misinformation. Her hands came up, strong hands with long narrow fingers, and touched my face and the experience was so startling in its clarity that I could actually feel her fingers pressing lightly just above my cheekbones, and when I looked out from the image I realized it was the old woman's hands on my face, and I jumped back, confused and horrified.

'How interesting.' Her voice was light and without inflection, like someone blowing gently through a tube.

The face reappeared for an instant in my head, in ripples, indistinct.

And then it was gone, and the witch had her fingers wrapped round the salt so I could no longer see it, and she looked at me and nodded, though I didn't say anything. I was back in the outside world, sitting at a table in the cafe while my tea grew cold.

Finn's witch stared at me and her face had a new dimension. Was it compassion? Pity? She shook her head, narrowed her eyes and pointed a gnarled finger at me, gently tapping the centre of my forehead.

'Look more carefully,' she said.

I blinked and realized that was it; that was my fortune. Trotting after her into the market, I wanted to ask questions, but she ignored me as thoroughly as if we'd never spoken.

Which brings me to my next rule, written with hindsight and a certain hard-won wisdom.

Rule number six: There are clues everywhere.

Finn arrived a minute later, and when we left, Witchy handed him his money, and sent him off with a wave. I might have been invisible.

'What's wrong?' Finn asked, nearly as soon as we set off. 'You look as if you've seen a ghost.'

I could have laughed at the appropriateness of the old cliché, but the ability to see the funny side had temporarily deserted me. I wanted to tell him about the uninformative fortune and the strange floating image, but I waited and waited for the right moment and for some reason it never came.

We walked briskly in the pale light, travelling single file along the footpath that skirted the school gates. Pale furled leaves and dazzling sunshine scoured my brain of dark visions. When we reached the water, the ebb tide was running strong, but instead of the kayak, Finn dragged a little dinghy out of its hiding place. I hadn't seen it before and despite its advanced state of disrepair, I was touched that he had considered the fact that there would be two of us crossing, and prepared for it – concrete evidence that I had entered his consciousness at a time when I was not actually standing in front of him. A thrilling discovery – like seeing a chimp make tools.

I helped him pull the heavier boat down from the dunes, wondering how hard it had been for him to get it up there in the first place. He stowed my bag in the bow while I clambered in as gracefully as possible, squinting into the sun. Finn pushed off, waded in a little and stepped lightly over the side, picking up the oars as he settled. The land rushed away from us at speed; all he had to do was steer in the direction of the little peninsula. The tide swept us out towards the sea, and then suddenly the momentum stopped and we were out of the current, becalmed. With a few lazy pulls of the portside oar, Finn guided us slowly to shore and I scrambled out to help him drag the boat up behind the shack.

My whole being was focused on trying to remain cool, pretending that spending two weeks without adults, without school, without authority or structure of any kind with my best (my only) friend was an ordinary occurrence. Impossible, of course. My head and stomach felt odd, my hands trembled, I had forgotten how to speak normally and was too agitated to eat.

Finn never seemed to notice my failures of poise, which surprised me. I had never in my life entered a room without instantly forming an impression of what everyone in it was doing and thinking. It was as natural as breathing to me, and I wondered if his ignorance were wilful.

The menu that night featured Finn's fish stew (stew, I had learnt, was his main area of culinary expertise), dished into large bowls with a teacup in lieu of a ladle. I could make out potatoes, carrots, crab, mussels and a mix of fishes, but suspected they were only the beginning; all manner of monsters were routinely dredged up from the bottom of the sea and served for tea courtesy of my host. But it tasted excellent.

The sense of occasion was such that we carried our food outside and ate leaning against the front of the house in the late golden light with the gentle lapping of waves in the background. Finn's little cat hung around, curling up on his lap for warmth. As I sat and tried to eat, my nerves seemed to flow out with the sea and I began to feel calm.

We sopped up the end of the stew with bread and sat back, sated, with no one to insist on prayers or protocol, and nothing at all to do before the next course, if we decided to have one.

When it came time for dessert, I brought out a cake, the last one left in the bakery, this time decorated with a clown in blue and green icing. I pulled the clown's head off and used a blunt knife to cut the cake into more or less wedge-shaped chunks. Finn accepted his without enthusiasm, having lived for years without jam and sweets, but for me, at that moment, cake had no equal on earth.

Licking icing off my fingers, I asked about our assault on the fort. I knew it would require an early start to hit the tide right. We didn't want to fight a vicious current on top of everything else.

'We won't have long,' Finn said, 'but we might catch a glimpse of it.' He seemed excited by the possibility, like a child, and I revelled in this unexpected show of enthusiasm.

We sat for a long time in the dark, watching the beam of a lighthouse flash, hypnotic and reassuring, accompanied by the toll of a buoy. The tide seemed particularly low tonight; the beach stretched far away from us and the waves lapped quietly in the distance. I guessed it had to do with the full moon.

'Is it true that you can still hear bells under the sea?' My question referred to the legend, popular at school, that the bells of the churches from the lost city could be heard on quiet summer nights. Naturally, I was convinced of the absurdity of such a notion.

'Of course,' Finn said, without turning his head.

I looked at him sideways to see if he was serious, but

nothing in his face offered a clue. For the next half-hour, until the temperature dropped and drove us inside, we sat in silence. I listened as hard as I could for the magic, but heard nothing but the clang clang clang of a buoy.

17

The sound of Finn boiling water woke me at dawn. He wasn't much for talking, especially at that hour, and wouldn't answer any conversation I initiated. Like the hut, he warmed up slowly, and I had a feeling his habit of solitude had existed for so long that it surprised him every morning to find me asleep where his granny had once lain.

It occurred to me that I had been at boarding school for a good many more years than Finn had lived alone, so perhaps my social skills were a little on the odd side as well. Whenever I was at home, I watched my mother chat brightly over breakfast the way an anthropologist might note typical social behaviour of the human species.

I hated getting up in the cold, and slept buried up to my eyes in blankets, removing them only to wrap my hands round a warm cup of tea. Finn had added sugar to mine unprompted and I turned away to hide my flush of pleasure. I knew that if I waited in bed for him to build up the fire and perform his morning tasks, the hut would gradually fill with a kind of fuggy warmth, so I lay still, savouring the familiar sounds and postponing re-entry into full consciousness for as long as possible.

Nothing in my life so far compared with those first minutes of the day, half-sitting in bed, still swaddled in warmth and with no imperative to move, just staring out of the window as the first pale streaks ignited the sky. I watched boats chug slowly past the windows: fishing boats returning from a long night of work, sailing boats from the nearby estuary taking advantage of the favourable tide, little tugs on their way back to port. At night passenger ships twinkled on the horizon like stars, but the daylight made them invisible.

'We'll take the dinghy,' Finn said over his shoulder, heading out of the door. Through the window I watched him go, watched his outline soften and blur as he disappeared into the morning haze. The world had not yet come into focus. Even the sound of the sea seemed muffled, as if heard from a long distance away. From where I sat it was nearly invisible, lost in a cloak of grey mist. I knew this moment of half-light wouldn't last, that in less than an hour daylight would have burned off the fog and restored the shape of things.

When I finally dressed and joined him, he was outfitting the little boat for our expedition: a wooden mast and sail retrieved from the dunes, a long coiled rope, a tin for bailing, an anchor. The sun blazed down and I knew that my thick jersey would soon feel uncomfortably warm.

Finn hauled up the little sail, swung the boat into the wind and pointed to where he wanted me. I climbed in at the bow and with a push and a jolt we were off, Finn handling the tiller and sail, and me singing pirate songs and 'What Shall We Do with the Drunken Sailor?' to amuse him.

He frowned at me. 'I'm doing all the work while you sit there making a horrible noise.'

'Yes,' I said happily, delivering a lusty chorus at twice my usual volume.

Finn grimaced. 'Come on, let's switch over. That ought to shut you up.'

'I can't sail.'

'I'll teach you.'

And suddenly there it was. The smile.

Awkwardly, we swapped places. Finn handed me a rope and a length of tiller and told me to hold both steady. 'Feel for the balance between them,' he told me.

I had no idea what he meant, and at first I struggled against wind and waves with every ounce of strength I possessed. To no avail. We proceeded in fits and starts, jerking along like an old car in the wrong gear, stopping and starting and swinging awkwardly left and right. Finn leant back and focused on the middle distance, smiling a little and refusing to help, and just as I was ready to give up, our forward motion turned tight and clean and straight and suddenly, against all expectation, we were sailing. *I was sailing!* The little boat sped along and together we soared, with the slap of the sea against the bow, the wind coming over the port side nearly in front of us, the sail taut as a trampoline. Speed and a slim wedge of terror made me reckless, ecstatic, for the three or four minutes it took before I headed the boat up too close to the wind and lost hold of the tiller. My moment of oneness with wind and sea ceased. The momentum of the boat jammed the tiller up into the far corner of the stern where I couldn't hope to reach. I hung on to my rope for dear life, despite the fact that the boat was now tipped up at a terrible angle, hurtling along, taking water in over the side.

'Let go of the sail!' I could hear Finn shouting, but my limbs had gone rigid, my eyes half-shut in a paralysed prayer for salvation, my hands locked obstinately around the rope. It took an almighty heave for him to pull the line from my hands and set it free, which had the magical effect of flattening the boat almost instantly. The tiller, suddenly loose and friendly, swung gently into his hand, and with a few minor adjustments we were sailing once more. He motioned me back to my place at the bow, uncharacteristically triumphant. If I hadn't known better I might have suspected him of proving a point: something about the very thin line between positive forward motion and chaos, panic, death.

Then again, maybe not.

Trying to think inside Finn's head was like committing what our English master called Pathetic Fallacy, the attribution of human emotions to boulders or trees. Finn was more likely thinking about the not-so-thin line between someone who knew how to sail and someone who didn't.

But I harboured no ill feelings; ballast was a role I embraced happily. By now the wind had picked up and I leant over the side, hypnotized by the flashes of sunlight on the dark sea as it rushed under our bow, by its green-black opacity. We'd been sailing north along the coast, out less than an hour, and already I'd forgotten our goal.

'Look there.' Finn pointed left at a shallow cove

surrounded by collapsing cliffs – great shelves of chalk and clay sliding down on to the beach. 'That's where the habour was.' I turned to look, squinting to focus better, while he neatly changed direction, angling the boat away from the shore.

We were about three hundred yards off the beach when suddenly I could see something ahead, something dark and looming just above the water line. I pointed, but Finn had already altered our course. As we approached I could see that it was man-made, but by the time I recognized it as the fort, the sea was trying to smash us to smithereens against it. Finn steered hard and swung us round the rampart as if it were a racing marker, an uncharacteristically reckless move, I thought, on the chance that there was substantially more Roman fort just under the surface.

It sounds like one of those horrible clichés, but this barely visible construction of two-thousand-year-old stone made the hairs rise on the back of my neck. Ever the romantic schoolboy, I suppose I'd been expecting something pristine: light grey walls carved into tidy castellations like a plastic play-castle in the bath. But the reality of it was heavy and dark and shaped like a thing from a nightmare, covered in barnacles and seaweed, and so low in the water that it was nearly invisible except when the sea parted between waves and the light caught it a certain way.

Fantasies I'd nursed about tossing a rope over a tower and stepping out of the boat to explore were laughable. The treacherous surge of the sea against those massive walls made such thoughts absurd. The only form of life that might cling to them belonged to limpets and mussels.

Finn had removed us to a safe distance and now we drifted, the sail soft and luffing, spilling wind while we mulled over our position.

He cocked his head at me, eyes sparkling with reflected sunlight. The corners of his mouth rose slightly, and if he could have leant back and crossed his arms over his chest, I think he would have.

'Well,' he said, 'there's your fort.'

There it was indeed. I strained for some sign of St Oswald's monastery, the tiniest remnant of cloisters and arches perched on top of the leviathan. But if such a thing had ever existed, there was no sign of it now.

Finn looked at me and shrugged. 'What next?'

Back at the hut that morning, safe in my warm bed, I had imagined slipping over the side of the boat and diving down, feeling my way along the smooth stone sides to the bottom, miraculously holding my breath until I neared the bottom, where a golden goblet and a crown would lie wafting softly in the sunlit sea, waiting for me to pluck them out and deliver them to Finn. I could see myself breaking back through the surface, spouting water like a whale and tossing the priceless treasure casually into the bottom of his boat as an offering.

But only a serious death wish could get me into the water now. With no clouds to muffle the wind, it flew round us, smashing waves against the ancient walls with a deep hollow *boom*. It was hard to believe those walls still held up against the sheer weight of cold black sea.

The sea had been hurling itself at the masonry minute by minute, hour by hour, day by day, for more than a thousand years and it made me wonder about the Romans, how they had managed to build walls so strong. And how had the barbarians breached the defences so easily? 'Easily' was how the history book described it, and I wondered if the person writing those words had ever seen a Roman fort close-up.

'Let's go,' I said. 'I've seen enough.'

Finn swung the boat away. The wind was behind us now, and he let the sail out all the way, cleating the mainsheet, and sitting back with the tiller under one arm. We flew over the water; our speed wonderful and terrifying. 'Changed your mind about exploring?' He had to shout to be heard.

'It wasn't what I expected.' I was glad the wind made conversation difficult.

'Do you want to have a look at the lost city? It's still early.'

I nodded and watched the smooth muscles in his arms as he brought the boat about. He was neither big nor particularly muscular, but agile and deft, able to convert the power of the sea, the wind, and the momentum of the boat into acceleration. Physics made easy.

I stared down into the water, hoping to catch sight of a fish swimming past. Finn slowed again and pointed at the shore. Through the scrubby trees growing out of the cliff, I could see the remains of what had once been an abbey perched high above the beach.

'We'll have a look around here,' he said, leaning over

with his face a few inches underwater. Half a minute later he surfaced, spluttering. The water was freezing, and it took a few tries before I managed to get used to its murky density. I plunged my head into the dark silent world, holding my breath till I thought my lungs would burst.

I saw nothing. Not a thing. No ruined city, no piece of a ruined city. No church or town hall or burgher's manse, not even a bloody fish. Just the cold, cold depths of the dark, dark sea. I felt sick with disappointment, worse than sick when I remembered what the witch had said about my future. Look more carefully? At what? I was searching with every fibre of my being and there was nothing to see.

Bugger the city, I thought, and bugger Finn's witch.

I was about to haul myself back up into the boat when I thought I glimpsed something. There wasn't much air left in my lungs but I turned my head to where the image appeared. Whatever it was or had been, it was gone. Yet something lingered on my retina like a photographic negative, a pale oval with streaming hair, fleeting and bright as the moon.

Jerking out of the water, I ducked my face into the crook of one elbow for warmth. 'Let's go,' I mumbled, without looking up. But then I heard Finn laugh, saw him soaked and dripping, and realized I'd been had. No mysterious vision then. Just him.

I growled and he made a 'hmph' noise like a camel, unaccustomed to any show of defiance by his lackey. But when I lowered my arm and raised my eyes, and he saw the blotchy face, the comic twist of mouth, the dripping hair and red nose, he smiled. It was a smile that might have expressed affection or amusement or something entirely else.

With the wind blowing full across the stern, we sailed for home.

18

I studied Finn the way some other boy might have studied history, determined to memorize his vocabulary, his movements, his clothes, what he said, what he did, what he thought. What ideas circulated in his head when he looked distracted? What did he dream about?

But most of all, what I wanted was to see myself through his eyes, to define myself in relation to him, to sift out what was interesting in me (what he must have liked, however insignificant) and distil it into a purer, bolder, more compelling version of myself.

The truth is, for that brief period of my life I failed to exist if Finn wasn't looking at me. And so I copied him, strove to exist the way he existed: to stretch, languid and graceful when tired, to move swiftly and with determination when not, to speak rarely and with force, to smile in a way that rewarded the world.

Of course in the most basic of ways, being Finn didn't suit me. I was slow and clumsy; uncomfortable in my own body. I lacked the ability to tolerate silence. I was lazy. Self-conscious. Unspontaneous.

There were twelve days left of Easter break.

Very early on Wednesday morning, well before sunrise, Finn headed up the beach with his ocean fishing rod to the mouth of the river, where wheeling seagulls the night before had informed him that the minnows were running. The courageous throwing off of blankets didn't faze him, but I hated it. It was bad enough on a cold morning in a miserable dormitory room. But in the early spring cold of a hut where you know that even the ordinary pleasure of an early morning visit to the toilet will bring your nether regions into direct contact with the wind off the North Sea? Practically impossible. So while I lay in bed, warm and snug and utterly content not to be dragged up and out by breakfast or chapel or lessons, Finn chose his lures and set off.

It was nearly an hour before I joined him, lazy and slow, but in the end unwilling to allow him any fragment of a life without me. In the grey light of early dawn, he cast his line off the beach where the river spat tiny fish out into the sea to flounder and die, attracting bigger fish to an easy meal. Patient and silent, he flipped his lure out over the water and reeled it slowly back in. I listened to the precise soft whir of the reel, watched the painted wood and feather decoy with its deadly armour of hooks become invisible, imagined it sinking down, languid and false, as Finn waggled it slowly back towards land. Hour after hour he repeated the exercise, patiently thinking his thoughts. It wasn't the most exciting form of entertainment, but I didn't mind. I was hypnotized by the simple grace of whatever it was he did and however it was he did it.

Huddled down into my jersey, dreamy and absent, I sat

and watched the sun glow pink and rise out of the sea, when unexpectedly there was a hand on my arm and a nod of the head in the direction he'd been casting.

I looked up, startled. The surface of the sea scrambled and boiled in a circle about thirty feet across, and I wondered if it heralded the appearance of our own private leviathan. As my eyes grew accustomed to the scene, I could see the outlines of fish and parts of fish, tails and fins and whole bodies occasionally hurtling out of the water and falling back again with a little splash.

'Herring,' Finn whispered happily, substituting a lighter rod for the one he'd been using, baiting it quickly and flipping his hook so it landed in the centre of the teeming circle. On his third cast, the rod twitched and bent over and he reeled the line in carefully, producing a shining silver and blue fish as long as his forearm. It fought like a weasel all the way to the beach.

I watched him kill it, watched him catch six more in quick succession before the boiling circle moved out of range. With great care and precision he gutted and cleaned each fish, slitting the belly and sweeping out the insides, then scraping the scales off backwards with a rasping noise. They flew off, landing on the beach where the rays of the half-risen sun made them glitter like sequins. They looked so beautiful that I picked one up, but in my hand it became a lifeless thing, slimy and disgusting.

He concentrated on his work and never once looked at me.

Finn made money selling fish in town, so we didn't eat them, but wrapped them in seaweed to be delivered later that day. In the meantime, we collected clams for lunch from a tiny cove in the estuary where they lived deep in the muddy clay. We waded barefoot and felt for them with our feet, reaching into the icy water to dig them up. My hands and feet quickly went numb as I dug the fat little creatures out and tossed them into a bucket. The blood from various scrapes and cuts ran unnoticed down my hands, leaving long pink streamers in the sea. Later I scrubbed the clams clean, and Finn threw them in a pot to steam with seawater and handfuls of bright green samphire from the marsh. The clams were salty and full of sand, but we wiggled the little bodies in hot water first to clean them, then dunked them in melted butter, sopping up the gritty butter with bread when we were done.

I kept waiting for the effect of this castaway existence to mark me somehow, make me more of a man, but as the hours and days slipped away I felt the distance between us increasing. The longer we spent together the more difficult it became to engage him in conversation. His silences grew, it seemed to me, became deeper, more remote. By Friday I had come to the conclusion that I was crowding him, so I made myself as small as possible, stifled the desire to burble over with enthusiasm for each new discovery or to follow him around like the adoring hanger-on I was.

An image of Reese crept into my brain and I cringed.

I became furtive, a silent, dismal being with nowhere to go and no permission to stay. This wasn't how I had imagined our time together, and whatever vision I'd had imagined for myself – heroic and handy, living rough off the land – was countered by the reflection I saw in his eyes.

Next time, I stayed behind when he went to market with his fish. I huddled in a corner, staring at the huge old history book, my eyes glazed with tears. I dozed for an hour or so, and it was cold and nearly dark when I heard the scrape of the kayak behind the hut. Jerking into a seated position, I threw off the blanket and opened the book to a random page, studying it with enough false intensity to pretend I hadn't heard him come in. Not that such posing was likely to have fooled him. My face, creased and flushed with sleep, betrayed me like a beacon.

He entered without greeting, and began stowing supplies in the kitchen.

'How was town?'

He looked up as if noticing me for the first time, considered the question and shrugged.

'I just meant . . .' And then the real words burst out, all in a rush. '*I'll go if you want me to.*'

Finn looked up at me, silent and closed, and I heard a horrible noise, wet and hollow, as something inside of me collapsed. Finally he shrugged, and in a tone more puzzled than hostile, said, 'Go if you want to.'

I turned away. 'I don't want to.'

'So?' He frowned.

'You want me to go.' My voice dropped to a whisper. 'I'm sorry, this isn't how I meant to be.' Halfway through this confession my voice broke.

Finn stared and shook his head. Then he left the room and went into the kitchen to build up the fire. Though unable to see and unwilling to wipe my eyes on my sleeve (the too-obvious gesture of a crying person), I could follow his movements as he chose a dry log and placed it carefully on to the bed of hot embers. Once the log began to crackle, he filled the kettle and placed it on top of the stove.

I turned away and began to gather my few belongings blindly, wondering what I would do and where I would go, imagined myself stooped and stumbling like Adam, wreathed in sin and expelled from paradise.

The riveting nature of my own self-pity distracted me so thoroughly that for a moment I forgot about Finn. When I looked up and saw him standing in front of me, I jumped a little.

There was a moment of silence during which he just stared: at the rumpled bed, the open history book, the socks and jersey and gloves scattered on the floor of the tiny house. *His* house, inviolate and solitary until now. I flushed and bent over like a supplicant, scuttling around to gather up the signs of habitation, to stuff them into my schoolbag, to erase myself completely from the scene.

Finn exhaled what might have been a sigh, then crossed over and began to climb the narrow staircase to his little room under the eaves. Halfway up he stopped and turned back to me.

'Actually,' he said, with an expression that was not meant to reassure, 'I quite like having you around.'

19

In the Dark Ages, most of life took place out of doors: the planting, herding, cooking, the buying and selling, the weddings, births, deaths, wars. In Finn's version of life in the twentieth century, not much had changed. Despite the cold, we walked and fished, lay on the beach and stared at the sunlit clouds or the stars in the night sky, pulled in the traps, messed about in boats. We walked to market with his fish or his bag of crabs and, like the Angles and Saxons, exchanged these commodities for things we didn't have – a hammer, a loaf of bread, a pair of woollen socks.

After only ten days at the hut I could appreciate the advantages of such a world, a world with nothing extra or unnecessary in it. A cooking pot, a place to sleep, a friend, a fire – what more did I require?

I loved the simple richness of our domestic life, the overlapping rhythms, the glancing contacts, the casual-seeming but carefully choreographed dance played out through the rooms of a shared house. I even learnt to accept Finn's silence for what it was and not read it as a reproach. It was a lesson that has proved valuable in later life, this acceptance of another person's silence, for I am more the silence-filler sort of person, hopeless on birdwatching expeditions. Despite the effort required to adapt, I became accustomed to whole days or parts of days during which we barely spoke, just drifted side by side in what for me was a dreamy silence, filled with unspoken words that slipped out of my brain and floated up to dissipate in the cold blue sky.

I began to pick up some of Finn's jobs, shovelling sand into the latrine, fetching water from the open tank at the far end of the huts. Neither of us commented on my expanded role, but I could read expressions on Finn's face that I might not have noticed before, slight shifts of the eyes or movements of the corners of the mouth. Pleasure. Displeasure. Impatience. And very occasionally: interest, amusement. Sometimes I believed I could chart the passage of thoughts across his face, though the content of those thoughts remained a mystery to me, as if written in another language.

For the rest of my break we lived together in a boyish ideal (*my* boyish ideal) of perfect happiness. I became used to the feel and the taste of my own salty skin. My face turned brown from exposure all day to the April sun, and for once in my life my hair felt thick, textured with salt. There was no mirror in Finn's hut, so I could look at him and imagine myself each day growing taller and slimmer and bolder. It was a lie in ways I already suspected, and ways I hadn't yet imagined. But it made me happy, and even then I knew that happiness was something in which to plunge headlong, and damn the torpedoes. Our time together would have to end, I knew that, and knew also that the pain of leaving this place would be intolerable, like death.

In all the years that followed, I have longed, sometimes quite desperately, to ask Finn about those weeks, to ask whether they were happy only for me, whether they remained vivid only in my head. I have wanted to ask whether my presence caused any change for the better. *Any change at all*. But I couldn't ask. It was once again the supplicant in me, the endlessly repentant me who wanted somehow to know that it had all been worthwhile, that destruction and ruin wasn't all I brought to the little house by the sea.

20

I returned to school, hoping I'd managed to get away with my Easter adventure, but there was a niggling sense of not-quite-rightness from the very beginning that stank of Reese. He skulked around, more malevolent and cringing with each passing day, and there was something about his Gollum act that struck me as too knowing. But like Reese himself, it was more convenient to ignore. So I did.

We were studying the four forces in physics, and as I pretended to grapple with these concepts, my mind wandered first to Finn, most graceful and mysterious of forces, then to rumour, which is a force in a league all its own.

Rule number seven: All rumours are true.

If you have the patience to wait and watch, history will reshape truth (weakest of all forces, and weightless) in the image of opinion. What really happened will cease to matter, and eventually, cease to exist.

The rumours claimed sightings of me in town and at the beach while I was meant to be on holiday with my family.

The interesting thing about these sightings is that they

were, in the main, invented. Not that this altered the essential truth that I was with Finn when I was supposed to be in Spain with my parents. Rumour, muddled up with gossip, painted me in the company of an older man (read: dirty old pervert) at various upmarket establishments around town, taking tea or digging into a duck breast with redcurrant sauce at The Ship Hotel while my consort licked his lips and slid his hand helplessly up my thigh.

It was the hackneyed quality of the tale that gave it credence; after all, it was well known that many of our schoolmasters were middle-aged bachelors with a yen for the extramural companionship of younger boys, and many perfectly respectable married gentlemen in town thought back on the sexual peccadilloes of their own schooldays with something closer to nostalgia than unease. Add this to the frustrations and privations of an all-male boarding school, a small town no longer connected to London by a train line, a part of the world in which winters were long and lonely and devoid of more wholesome distractions, and you had the perfect setting for perversion – of truth, at the very least.

The accusations began as whispers, and most were so far off the mark that I didn't bother to deny them. I might have missed them altogether if it hadn't been for Reese, reporting back on all the latest stories as if he had nothing to do with bringing them to life. But by Wednesday of that first week, the jeering had emerged from the closet (so to speak) and come to the attention of my housemaster. A summons was duly made and received, and at 2 p.m. the following afternoon, in the break between cadet drill and

RE, I trudged over to the Gothic brick gatehouse where Clifton-Mogg kept an office, and knocked (with a forthright, innocent knock) on the door.

'Come in,' he called, with that perfect mix of kindness and authority meant to seduce confidences and bring about the collapse of will.

I entered his study and he ignored me for long minutes, another old trick for prolonging the agony (the curiosity, the worry, the guilt). It had the opposite effect on me. As he scribbled notes, my heartbeat slowed, my tendency to babble dried up. I became Finn, steely, resolved.

'Did you have a pleasant holiday?' He didn't look up.

'Yes, sir. Quite pleasant.'

'Majorca, was it?'

'Yes, sir.'

'Chilly this time of year, wasn't it?'

How should I know? 'Not very,' I said cautiously. 'Warmer than here, anyway.'

Mr Clifton-Mogg grunted.

My parents had indeed gone to Spain for Easter and enjoyed themselves greatly. I knew this from the letter I received on my return from Finn's.

'There is talk,' he began, looking up at last and speaking slowly, lips pursed with disapproval. 'There is talk' – he repeated the words for emphasis – 'that you were sighted in town during the holiday break.'

There *is* talk. You *were* sighted. Despite his many faults, Thomas Thomas had managed to impress upon us the importance of avoiding the passive tense in our spoken and written work. It denoted weakness. This weakness (combined with the fact that Clifton-Mogg had posed no direct question) gave me the confidence to execute a king's gambit.

I said nothing.

Clifton-Mogg glanced away, a peevish note in his profile – uncertainty, perhaps? 'Well?' he said at last. 'What do you have to say to these accusations?'

Accusations, suddenly?

With the perfect composure of the pathological liar, I looked him straight in the eye, unblinking. 'I was with my parents, sir. You're welcome to phone them up and ask.'

He stared at the board as I exposed my queen.

It was a gamble, certainly, but not as real a gamble as you might imagine. With no hard evidence and no confession to go on, Clifton-Mogg was stumped. I knew it and he knew it. He couldn't simply phone my parents and ask whether I'd really gone with them to Spain during the break; it would amount to a blatant confession that the school had no clue where the boys in its charge spent their time, and furthermore, that it had taken this many weeks to discover the extent of their irresponsibility.

Checkmate.

He sighed again.

'Very well. Assuming your parents are happy to confirm your whereabouts, we needn't discuss the matter again.'

But I knew he wouldn't take up the matter with my parents. I held his gaze, modestly triumphant, and he looked away.

'Now.' Here he cleared his throat, as if getting to the real reason for our meeting. 'Tell me, how are you getting along this term generally?'

I nearly laughed out loud. 'Fine, sir.' And then, lowering my voice to an earnest drone, 'I want to do well.' My eyes met his, pupils dilated with conviction.

He cleared his throat again. 'Excellent. We often succeed with boys like you where others have failed. It's rather a point of pride.'

Ah, the platitudes of a long, uncontroversial career.

'Good food and brisk exercise of body and mind. Never fails. Right then. Off you go.' He consulted a large chart in front of him on the desk. 'RE, is it? Tell Headmaster I kept you.'

I bowed my head, muttered 'Thank you, sir,' and scarpered, my feet swift and light with relief. I felt like launching into a wild dance, but instead, practised my impersonation of a schoolboy keen to get back to work, my face set in a mask of humility.

Beneath the mask, I grinned.

21

My triumph didn't last. I was being watched, I was sure of it. The school suspected illicit behaviour and was out to prove it, determined to thwart any idea I had of escaping, if only for an hour or two. The campaign was infuriatingly subtle and effective – they couldn't restrict me from leaving school grounds because, technically, I'd done nothing wrong. But, along with a number of my classmates, I found myself volunteered into service for the drama club – working evenings and weekends on the school's summer term presentation of *The Importance of Being Earnest*.

My partner? Who else but Reese.

Thereafter, every spare moment was spent converting school desks into Chippendale escritoires with the help of plywood and paint. We painted thousands of dummy book spines on to cardboard and stapled them in rows on wooden armatures representing bookcases, mounted drawing-room doors on wheels for the scene change and used cardboard and papier mâché to construct a grand piano from the miserable tuneless wreck in the music room. I kept myself separate from the fray, toiling for hours painting unnecessary titles on to the spines of books with a tiny paintbrush, and more hours on a grand ancestral portrait of Algernon's grandfather (historically accurate down to the curl of the moustache, but cartoonishly awful nonetheless).

I didn't mind working on props as much as I thought I would. It was something to do, after all, and the approval rating we got for mucking-in far outweighed the effort required. I couldn't have cared less about the production itself, though we had a fine Lady Bracknell with a great shelf of a bosom played by a senior boy, James Aitken. He was tall and fair-haired with a talent for rugby and an inability to hide his excitement at wearing ladies' clothing. He couldn't act, but his figure in a Victorian gown gave every syllable an unintentional comic flourish that would prove a great success on the night.

At first I refused to respond to Reese's attempts at conversation, but as time wore on I gave in. Finn wasn't exactly chatty, and more to the point, I couldn't talk to him about the subject I was most interested in, namely *Finn*. Being horrible to Reese, on the other hand, took quite a bit of effort given how much he seemed to like me, and I flattered myself that he'd keep our conversations secret because I told him to.

The confessions all went one way – I'm ashamed to say I never asked him a thing about himself – and it wasn't exactly an unburdening of the heart. I told him about the boy in the hut, describing him as impossibly heroic, and myself only slightly less so. As I indulged in the ecstasy of *telling someone*, I heard myself building an elaborate fiction around our already-glorious pursuits. In my stories we built slingshots and rafts, hunted deer and sailed to

Holland. The idea of having to exaggerate what was already the most amazing story of my life makes me sad for my former self. But Reese's awe made the fiction irresistible, and he was as close a friend as I was ever likely to have at St Oswald's, despite the fact that I couldn't stand him.

Rule number eight: Trust no one – least of all yourself.

Between rehearsals and preparation for exams, I was too tired even to think about plotting escape. But nights were another story. There, in the dark, nothing stopped my mind from returning to the place I was happy. In my dreams I didn't need lies. My imagination conjured Finn's salty woodsmoke smell, and filled in the spaces between us.

In the harsh light of day, I wondered whether Finn missed me, or felt hurt that I hadn't been to see him. Part of me revelled in my role of prisoner, always with the vain hope that it might be a punishment for Finn as well. Without admitting it, even to myself, I lived in hope that a sign would somehow arrive, a note addressed to me in unfamiliar handwriting, a request to meet.

But there was nothing.

Until one day I could stand it no longer. On Friday morning, with the dress rehearsal weekend looming, with exams in seven subjects just two weeks away and an epidemic of glandular fever raging through the school, I queued to see matron and obtain a sick note, an excuse to stay in bed all day Friday. Such notes were not easy to come by; matron could detect a fabricated symptom from half a mile away. But with so many feverish, red-throated boys congregating outside her little medical room, she barely had time to examine us all, and I took the extra precaution of running the long way round to get there, arriving splotchy, red-faced and overheated. She barely glanced at my throat.

'Here,' she said with a sigh, scribbling on her blue pad, 'here's your note. There's nothing for it short of bed rest. I'll see you again on Monday and for God's sake, don't kiss anyone.' She glanced at me with a malicious little smile, repeating the joke she'd probably made a hundred times already that week. And yet I couldn't help wondering if even she'd heard the rumours.

With gritted teeth and half-shut eyes, I made a great show of dragging myself to my feet, staggering a little at the doorway. Acting? Ha. Compared with Lady buggering Bracknell, I was Lawrence Olivier. Any minute now I'd be called to collect my award for best performance in the role of boy with non-specific symptoms of a useful alibi.

Luckily, my evil room-mates had not yet succumbed to the plague, and I waited, huddled and moaning slightly for effect, till they disappeared off to lessons the next morning.

'Lucky bastard,' from Gibbon was all they offered by way of sympathy, and, 'that's what you get for snogging old men.'

When I didn't answer, Gibbon loomed in close, nose to nose. 'You don't look ill to me.'

I kneed him in the groin and turned over to face the wall, leaving him to shriek agony and revenge from the floor until Barrett dragged him away. Reese lingered, his mouth opening and closing like a fish. In the end he too left.

By 8 a.m., with what was left of the healthy student body hard at work, I was out the front gate and partway down the footpath. Desperate though I was to see Finn, I didn't dare risk the road, and so hurried along, head down, behind the thin cover of trees. The sun might turn warm in a few hours, but for now I tucked my hands up into my armpits as I jogged along, hugging myself for comfort as much as for warmth.

When I arrived at the beach, the water was high. There had been no time for the niceties of a tide chart, and I muttered a prayer under my breath and trudged up into the dunes, hoping to find Finn's kayak.

It was there, neatly lashed to the old rusted winch. So Finn was either working or had left the boat for me on the off chance that I might get away. If only it were the latter. I prayed I'd find him at home, drinking tea or reading, that he'd look up calmly yet with barely disguised pleasure and say, 'Well, well. It's about time you showed up.'

The crossing blew treacherous with eddies, but I was no longer helpless in the kayak. I could balance fairly well, and knew how to use the currents to guide my little craft gently to the beach on the far side. Once there, I dragged the boat behind me to the hut and carefully secured it, drawing out the moment of anticipation. I noticed that the sea seemed to have advanced even in the few weeks since I'd last visited, the little waves washing up to within a few feet of the hut.

There was no sign of Finn through the windows, and no answer to my series of bold knocks.

I opened the door. The hut was empty and the fire just glowing ash, a sign that it had been left for some hours. I walked through the little house touching things gently, reminding them of my presence, rubbing up against Finn's life like the cat, reclaiming ownership. At a loss for what to do next, I built up the fire, set the kettle on the old stove and stood watching, waiting for it to boil. Which it did at last, despite the old adage.

With my tea I stepped out of the hut, scanning the shore and then turning towards the horizon, where fishing boats trailed seagulls like pennants. Nothing on earth could convince me the fisherman's life was a romantic one, what with the relentless rocking cold, the loneliness, the danger. Not to mention the killing. All those silvery bodies drowning in air. I went back inside and just sat, wondering what to do next.

The door opened.

'Thanks for stealing my boat.' He was shivering and dripping wet.

'Oh, God, I'm so sorry . . .'

But through chattering teeth he smiled and I felt that he really might have been pleased to see me. The water in the kettle was still hot and I turned into one of those cartoon figures racing about fetching things and talking at the same time, babbling apologies, and information about *The Importance of Being Earnest* and how I'd wanted to come sooner.

All the while Finn stood in the centre of the room,

dripping and strangely passive. His face was flushed, and when I handed him a towel I could feel the heat coming off him in waves.

'You don't look well,' I said, in a spirit of joviality rather than concern. 'Get changed and I'll make the tea.'

He nodded, turned, and began to ascend the stairs to his little loft, moving carefully, clumsy with cold.

Something in me hesitated, but I didn't stop to think. Even if I'd wanted to, I had no idea how to worry about Finn.

He'll be pleased to see me again, I thought, throwing myself wholeheartedly into the task of brewing tea. He'll be pleased to have someone make *him* a cup of tea for a change.

I made it thick and black and waited for him to reappear, working slowly, stalling a minute or two, adding a heaped teaspoon of sugar on my own initiative because of the chill, searching around in vain for a biscuit or a piece of cake, perhaps left over from my last visit. There'd been no time to bring supplies this time – I'd even thought (yes, a touch defiantly) that he'd have to take me as I was, without bribes and offerings for his favour. But now I regretted having nothing to give. It was my fault, after all, that he was freezing cold and soaking wet.

I shifted from foot to foot, impatient, a housewife having gone to all the trouble of making dinner and receiving no response from her family. I tried swallowing the silence along with my tea, glancing at the stairs occasionally, casually, where things seemed to have gone rather quiet.

'You haven't gone to sleep on me, have you?' I called

loud enough for him to hear but there was no answer. Frowning, I started across the room. 'Finn? I've got your tea.'

Silence.

I had never been upstairs. 'Finn?' The tremor in my voice betrayed nerves – about his failure to answer, and the possibility of having to breach the inner sanctum. I climbed a few steps. 'Finn?'

Panicked now, I took the stairs two at a time, splashing hot tea on the floor and walls, and found him lying on his bed under the eaves, his face chalky white. 'I'm OK,' he whispered, though clearly he wasn't. 'I haven't been feeling too well.' Even huddled under the blankets he was shivering. When he swallowed, he squinted with pain.

Oh, Lord. 'Hang on,' I yelped, running downstairs for the hot-water bottle. With trembling hands, I unscrewed the stopper and emptied the kettle into it, splashing my fingers with boiling water and cursing. There wasn't quite enough in the kettle to fill it, so I tipped in what was left of the tea and bounded back up the stairs, replacing the stopper as I went. It took some insistence to pry the blankets out of his fist and give him the warm rubber bottle to hug. In the process I noticed that he'd managed to pull on a dry shirt and jersey, but his legs were bare; he'd evidently collapsed before he could finish dressing. There was a small pine chest near the bed, and I pulled open drawers until in one I found a pair of flannel long johns. He struggled with me, embarrassed, and at last I bowed to his modesty and left him to wriggle into them himself.

What price dignity, I thought for a wry instant. And then, 'Have you got any aspirin?'

'Downstairs,' he croaked. 'In the red tin.' I found the tin, and rummaged through the ancient first-aid kit with its neatly rolled Second World War bandages, in search of something for pain. The thought that I had managed to infect him with glandular fever on my last visit did occur to me – we'd been told it could take weeks to incubate – but the fact was, *Finn did not get ill*. He had told me himself that he could not remember feeling unwell, ever. And yet perhaps I *had* infected him, perhaps I had carried the weapon into his life disguised as friendship, like the American settlers, bearing alcohol, the common cold, and other fatal trinkets.

An ancient pillbox was marked 'aspirin', and I guessed they were his gran's and about a hundred years old. Tipping out a handful, I poured a mug full of cold water and hurried back upstairs.

Finn shook his head when he saw the tablets and closed his eyes again, so I fetched a spoon and crushed them to powder, stirring until they dissolved in half an inch of water and placing it in his hand, firmly, like an Edwardian nanny. He managed to sit up a little and drink the foul mixture, grimacing. One more trip downstairs for the blankets off my bed and then I smoothed his covers and left him, eyes closed, breath peaceful.

Now what? I couldn't exactly go back to school and forget him. And what was the food situation? I kicked myself for not having brought anything, wondering if I could make it into town, back here and back to school without getting expelled. There was leftover porridge in a saucepan, a few days old at least, to which I added water, sugar and butter, then heated and stirred it to make a sloppy gruel. After that there was nothing for me to do but bank up the fire and collapse, no longer able to suppress the tremor in my limbs that came from being tired and stressed and chilled with responsibility I didn't want.

22

Finn slept and slept. It grew dark, and my fretting about the time took on an edge of panic. Unable to wait any longer, I woke him, and to my relief he seemed a little brighter.

'Could you eat something?' When he made a face, I adopted a brisk, no-nonsense voice. 'Of course you can, here, it's nice.' I practically forced the sweet porridge down him, spilling some on the bedclothes and some down his neck, and I think he ate just so he wouldn't have to lie in a puddle of the stuff after I left.

'Look, Finn,' I said, 'I've got to get back to school. But I'll come on Sunday with food and aspirin. In the meantime, I think you've got to move downstairs by the fire. That way there's not so far to go if you need anything.'

He nodded, and I helped him to his feet, supporting him awkwardly down the narrow stairs. Together we lurched and wove back and forth like Laurel and Hardy, and I couldn't help wondering if he'd have done a better job on his own. He sat in a chair while I returned for his bedding to make up the little alcove bed. Despite the warm day, I was cold with inactivity and fear.

I piled blankets on and smoothed a clean tea towel on the pillow for him as matron had done once when I had a sweaty fever. I even tucked him in. Despite the state of him, he seemed bemused by this reversal of roles, though I doubt he had the strength to resent my ministrations. I placed the bowl containing the rest of the warm porridge on the bookcase near his head, poured a tall glass of water, and glanced at my watch.

'OK.' I was brisk, efficient. Florence Nightingale, this time, with the soldiers of the Crimea. 'Anything else?'

He looked uncomfortable. 'A bowl, or . . .'

Of course! He wasn't about to trek out in the cold to the privy. I fetched the bucket and placed it carefully by the bed. 'That should keep you out of trouble.'

He didn't smile.

The fire banked, the patient swaddled and fed, there was no more excuse for me to hang about. The risk of eternal hellfire and damnation at the hands of Clifton-Mogg grew as the sun dropped towards the horizon, so I said goodbye and promised to return. Finn's eyes were closed and he seemed not to have heard.

The tide was lower now but not low enough to cross without the kayak. I hesitated, weighing up the various miseries that awaited me in my new role as hero (drowning, freezing, exposure to the elements and my schoolmasters), then decided to play safe by dragging the boat along. I was already criminally late, but it was better than swimming alone in the dark.

Adrenalin made me uncharacteristically strong and swift, and the journey went without incident, in record time. At the school gate, I encountered the music master, back from town with a parcel under one arm and a song, as usual, in his heart. He might not have noticed me (so absent was his mind from anything relating to the real world) if I hadn't greeted him in my best false-jovial manner.

Confused and a bit blustery, he puffed up his feathers like a chicken. 'Isn't it rather late for you to be out and about?' The way he asked the question made it clear he had no idea what the answer should be.

'Afternoon exeat, sir.' I reached into my pocket, pulled out my folded sick note, waved it vaguely in his direction, frowned a little, looked concerned. 'Our year's had them all term.' Respect seasoned with a touch of self-righteousness.

'Why yes, of course, fine,' he murmured, and fluttered off into the darkness, humming, relieved to be free of any reminder that he taught school for a living.

My room-mates didn't let me off so easily.

Barrett was first. Throwing himself over the edge of the partition wall, he gaped at me with mock horror. 'Holy Jesus, you've been *out all day*? You're a dead man. Exactly how much is my silence worth?'

But Barrett wasn't low enough to turn me in, and in any case morality wasn't his thing, extortion was. In minutes he was fixed up with his favourite dummy-substitute, exhaling slowly, pensively, filling the tiny room with smoke. Luckily there was no sign of Gibbon. Across the room, Reese stared at me with his creepy, knowing look. When I caught his eye, he actually winked. I felt sick.

'*Jesus*, Barrett.' Gibbon entered the room and I sighed,

wearily prepared for battle. 'At least open the bloody window before we choke to death.' Barrett answered with a plume of smoke blown full into Gibbon's face, at which Gibbon roared, picked up the nearest thing from the floor and hurled it at his adversary, scoring a bullseye to the left temple with Reese's shoe. A blazing row broke out, ending with the door barricaded and Gibbon locked out. For once the gods were on my side.

I slipped into bed, pulled a pillow over my head and disappeared from the present. I had my work cut out for me on Sunday, and no idea how I was going to pull it off.

23

You'll notice at this point that I hadn't really focused on Finn's being ill. There was something in me that refused to believe it was serious, was certain that when I showed up like the US cavalry, Finn would be up and going about his business, frowning and asking why I'd bothered to come. So secure was I in our relative roles.

I stumbled through the Saturday dress rehearsal, distracted and fidgety. Attendance at chapel the following morning was strictly enforced, and even if my housemaster hadn't missed me, Reese was watching like a hawk.

What a hero I was. Chapel first, then life and death. A few lusty verses of 'And Did Those Feet in Ancient Times' followed by 'He Who Would Valiant Be', or perhaps, in my case, *not* be. I made a quick calculation as to how long it would take to detour into town (ages), and what would be open (nothing), and decided on a raid of the house kitchen as the softer option. We'd all done it, you just had to get your timing right, coordinate breaking and entering with cook's breakfast, act quickly and without fear. In the meantime I shoved a few vital supplies into the pocket of my satchel (five bottles of pills), for once grateful that

Reese was the floor's biggest hypochondriac. I didn't bother worrying which pill did what; I could sort that out later. I also packed a pair of warm socks and a knitted hot-water bottle cover from Barrett's mum.

The door by the kitchen rubbish bins was always unlocked, which made the whole operation a bit like storming a church crèche. Look left, look right, stroll in. The kitchen was deserted except for Young Sammy, who had what nowadays are called Learning Difficulties, but what we called 'not all there'. He was chopping onions in the corner, looking cheerful despite the tears running down his face. I waved and he waved back. On the stone worktop, a heap of fatty pork awaited destruction by overcooking. I grabbed a couple of streaky slabs, enough for two or three meals at least, and shovelled them into my satchel. Nothing like books that stink of pork blood. Next stop was the larder, where a round Victoria sponge beckoned. I grabbed it, a second later adding another. They crumbled as I shoved them into my bag with the pork.

Footsteps. Ducking under the table, I folded myself in behind two rough wooden crates of veg and waited for the sound to pass, so bold I didn't bother to shiver in fearful silence, but reached in and continued stuffing my bag, with potatoes now, silently of course, as I could actually see Billy the Cook's legs from my hiding place. Night-time was better for raids, he was nearly always drunk and didn't care so much about his precious stockpiles, but I relied on the fact that his hearing wasn't much good any more thanks to five decades of shouting at Young Sammy, who must have been sixty by now. Billy lit a cigarette, tossed the flaming match on to the floor more or less by my feet, and left the kitchens grumbling his usual stream of discontent. The match continued to burn as I waited to make sure he hadn't changed his mind, perhaps begun (uncharacteristically) to worry about burning the school kitchens down. I wriggled out of my hiding place, crushing the tiny flame with my foot. Reluctantly, I admit. Every schoolboy dreams of conflagration.

What else? A handful of hard white sugar lumps from the supply for the master's table. *Sugar and cake and blood and pork. That's what little boys are made of.*

Oh, Christ, bread. Delivery didn't come till Monday morning, but there were a few leftover brown rolls in the bread bin.

I humped the satchel strap up across my chest, waved to Sammy and set off. Wished I'd had a balaclava and black leather gloves. I rather fancied myself in spy mode, what boy wouldn't?

Almost forgot the reason for my mission.

24

Finn was a little better. I arrived desperate for signs of wellness, desperate for any indication that he'd improved; that his fever had broken. It happened all the time, in old films – the patient sweating and pale, the distraught wife, cut to the night sky, the clouds break, the sky clears, the eyes of the patient open and a tearful voice murmurs, 'He's going to live!'

In my mediocre documentary, the patient just lay there looking pale, sweating and shifting his limbs constantly, as if moving this way or that would stop the ache in them.

'How are you?' I asked, unnecessarily.

His response was raspy. 'Fine.'

'You look lousy. Remember I told you about glandular fever at school? I think that's what you've got.' I didn't add that if it was, it was I who had infected him. He was probably bright enough to have reasoned that one out himself.

He looked at me dully and pointed to the glass of water I'd left him. It was empty. The bucket had been used. Not elegantly, I might add, I smelled urine when I entered the hut, and found it splashed on the floor.

There is great comfort to be had in an orderly sequence

of chores. Fire. Water. Food. Medicine. I attacked each job with complete absorption, as if each were the beginning and end of my responsibilities on earth.

Despite the gloominess of my tasks, outside was cool and clear and the room streamed with sunlight. I banked up the fire and returned to Finn, propped him up with a folded blanket and handed him a glass of water, holding it for him between sips.

In a jolly-hockey-sticks voice that I'm sure I'd only ever heard in *Carry On* films, I began to unpack my stolen booty, uttering the occasional 'look what we have here!' in what I imagined was a cheering tone. But Finn's eyes were mostly closed, and after a few embarrassing moments I took my travelling show off to the kitchen and busied myself out of his line of sight, putting the water on for tea while I considered what to do with the pork.

I couldn't believe Finn wasn't hungry; I guessed he hadn't eaten properly in days. I watched as he tried to drink, his shoulders hunched and tense. After a few sips, he shook his head, pushed the glass away, and the only thing I could get him to consider were Reese's pills. I sifted through them, reading the long names and indications on the labels with interest: *For diarrhoea. For constipation. For swelling. Three times a day. After meals. One at night as necessary.* One small bottle looked promising and I held it up for him to read: *Twice daily for pain (may cause drowsiness).* They were tiny, so I made him swallow two to be safe, and sure enough within twenty minutes he was asleep, a look of almost angelic repose on his face.

I didn't have much clue how to cook the pork, but I did

have a vague idea about broth. So before anything else, I covered the slabs with water and put them on to boil. It took a long time for the water to heat up, and when it did, the surface quickly filled with a foul-smelling greyish scum that I tried to scrape off with a spoon. I stuck a couple of rolls on the top of the woodstove, placed the less ruined of the two sponges on a plate and tried to rinse the blood out of the sugar lumps.

With everything more or less in order, I sat down next to Finn and watched him sleep. His features looked even more delicate than usual, his eyelids violet and nearly translucent. He had long lashes, like a girl's, and I couldn't help wondering how he'd manage with my sort of life. With his looks, his skill as an athlete, and his natural reserve, he might inadvertently end up top of the heap at St Oswald's, despite lacking all the requisite social guile. For some reason this thought annoyed me.

After an hour, the broth began to smell less disgusting. I boiled it further, added salt, took one of the partially burnt rolls off the stove, ladled the soup into a teacup and brought it to Finn. He was half-awake now, but didn't seem keen on eating, so I goaded and joked until he gave in, probably just for a bit of peace and quiet. Fire, water, food. The soup was fatty and rich, with bits of meat floating in it, a real Anglo-Saxon repast. He sipped slowly, shaking his head 'no' when I produced the bread roll. So I crumbled it up and added it to the soup, where it turned soggy and soft and went down more easily. Soon his eyes began to roll back, he pushed the cup away and in seconds had drifted back to sleep.

146

I opened a window to let in some fresh air. It was the ultimate luxury after a long winter of huddling and shivering. The smell of the sea sweetened the atmosphere in the hut and made me feel more optimistic. There wasn't much else I could do about the smell of urine.

It was early afternoon when Finn awoke, his throat dry and painful. 'Time for your tablets,' I sang like an idiot, but when I approached with the cup, he turned away from me. I prodded him gently. 'Come on, it'll help you feel better, there's a good boy.' For an answer he flung out one arm and knocked the cup out of my hand and across the room, where it narrowly missed the window, smashing against the wooden frame with a report like a rifle.

All the tension of the past few days exploded. 'What *the hell* are you doing? You think I'm here for the fun of it?'

'Well, go then! Who asked you to come here?' His voice was a furious croak and I wondered at the pain it cost him to shout at me. For an instant before he turned away again, I caught a glimpse of his face and it looked frightened.

I mopped up the soup, swept the pieces of china off the floor, and filled a new cup, finishing my chores silently with an air of dignified reproach. He could treat me as he liked; I wasn't going to give up on him. On the other hand, I felt no obligation to relinquish the moral high ground by telling him when I'd be back. It was cruel of me, but I gained a peculiar satisfaction from it. For the briefest of moments in our history together, I realized I was more important to him than he was to me.

The tide was high, and the sea surged against the foundation of the hut. I thought of ancient civilizations lying underwater, or stacked below the hut in uneven layers, the long-forgotten lives of fishermen, weavers, farmers. Finn's place in the universe was so fluid, he might have belonged to any one of those civilizations, any century leading up to this one. If I closed my eyes for a moment I could even imagine that he had come here through a blip in the universe, that while I was gone he would return (silently, gracefully) to his daub-and-wattle hut and slide easily back into an earlier, more savage world. That would suit him best of all, I thought. He didn't belong to an age of Disney and motor cars and compulsory education.

I didn't speak a word to him as I left.

25

On Monday, the day of the opening of our play, the weather turned glorious. All around, schoolboys emerged like tortoises from deep down in their coats, at first naked and pale and a little dazed, then leaping and running with the sheer exuberance of feeling sun on their skin.

I had lessons all day Monday, and a last-minute run through before dinner. The play went on at seven, and was considered a success despite a number of conspicuous prop failures: my portrait fell off the wall halfway through Act Three and Lady Bracknell's bosom broke free of its harness in the final scene, requiring poor Aitken to speak his final scenes with both hands supporting his cleavage. The effect was most unladylike, but with encouragement from the front rows, Aitken bounced his rubber assets so energetically that by the time the curtain came down, audience and cast had collapsed in joyous anarchy.

With the play on all week and a history essay to write, there was no possibility of escape before late afternoon on Wednesday, and even that meant skipping a meeting with my housemaster. There was nothing for it but to go to Finn and afterwards tell old Clifton-Mogg that I was ill, had forgotten, become so absorbed in medieval England that the hours had simply flown past.

I'd been stealing food from meals to avoid the necessity of another full-fledged kitchen raid, and had filled my satchel with apples, oranges, stale rolls, butter, half a ginger cake, four greasy sausages and a handful of teabags. I half expected to be followed around school by a line of rats.

The late afternoon shimmered with sunshine and for the first time I noticed that the hawthorn hedges were in bloom. The pungent combination of brine and warm soil filled my nostrils, and at one point I heard the whoosh whoosh whoosh of heavy wings and looked up in time to see a trio of giant white swans flying just above my head. Under other circumstances the vision would have filled me with joy.

Finn lay exactly where I'd left him seventy-two hours earlier, and whatever shreds of optimism I'd preserved turned to fear at the smell that hit me when I came through the door. I called his name but there was no answer. Oh, Lord, I thought, what if he's dead? But there was no one to appeal to for help so I approached the bed, trying not to breathe through my nose, and crouched next to him. His eyes flickered open.

'You scared me for a minute there.' I smiled encouragement, felt his head (which was hot), and retreated to build up the fire. The nights were windy and damp, and despite the sunny day, the hut felt uncomfortably cool without a fire. Once it was crackling away, I tapped out two more pain tablets, meaning to dissolve them in a little hot broth, but there was a thick layer of yellow fat in the large saucepan, so I gave them to him with cold water instead. He still hadn't spoken, but I consoled myself with the knowledge that glandular fever made its victims painfully ill, but wasn't the sort of disease that killed you if left untreated.

And the smell? I kicked myself for not having thought of the stack of blue-and-white enamelled bedpans in the San. But it was too late for that.

I approached the bed again, silently lifting a corner of the pile of blankets. My stomach lurched, I could taste vomit at the back of my throat, but I only had a second to see that the bedclothes were soaked and filthy before he struck out at me with what little strength he still possessed. I made a soothing noise and looked at him, but he wouldn't meet my eyes, and I wondered whether his lack of response had as much to do with embarrassment as anything else.

'Never mind,' I told him. 'You can have a bath when the water heats up.' It must have been awful for him, lying there in the bed full of shit and piss, but until the stove did its job, I wasn't going to touch him. I passed the time fetching coal from the bunker and stacking wood from the woodshed behind the hut. His cat, yowling, followed me around until I fed it a few small pieces of fatty pork. Take it or leave it, I sneered, in honour of old wounds.

The soup warmed up eventually and he managed to drink most of what was in the teacup. I left him to it and set about dumping saucepans filled with hot water into the tin washtub he used as a bath. It nearly emptied his water store and took forever to heat enough for a decent bath. My arms ached. We didn't speak; the excuse of his bad throat a relief.

I found a bar of soap by the sink and dropped it in, swooshing the warm water around until it made bubbles. 'OK, let's do it,' I said.

He shook his head.

'Come on, Finn.' Jesus, he was stubborn. 'I haven't got much time, and I'll have to make the bed again too.'

He croaked that he wanted a chair, and at last, with a sigh, I brought one over and left him to it. I guessed anyone living on his own for so long might be modest; I'd noticed before that he never took his clothes off around me. I was completely immune to such physical niceties, had been undressing in front of other boys all my life. I shrugged, went back into the kitchen, and left him alone for ten minutes or so, until the splashing noises stopped. A blanket draped over the chair hid him from me. 'Are you OK?' I called and he nodded. 'I'll get you a towel.' There were bubbles in the bath water and it had turned a horrible colour. I wasn't sure a person could get clean this way, but I supposed it would be an improvement. Upstairs I found clean flannel trousers, an old soft shirt, a woollen pullover and warm socks. Without looking, I placed them on the chair and held the towel out for him.

He took it. 'I'm OK now.' I turned away, and he wrapped himself in the towel and pulled on the shirt as I prepared to attack the bed.

'I'll do that,' he said, staggering slightly in an attempt to push me away.

'Oh, for the love of buggering Mary mother of buggering

Christ what is wrong with a little help? Just let me get on with it!' I scrabbled in the drawer under the bed for anything resembling clean sheets. I had a feeling it was thanks to his gran that a pile remained, carefully folded and smelling of smoke, unused all these years.

I pulled his sheets and blankets off the bed in a bundle, dumping them together on the floor, postponing the moment I would have to separate the soiled from the non-soiled. God, they stank. I kept my head politely averted while he dressed, and when I turned back, had to admit he looked better – the pills had lowered his fever, and despite soaking in a vat of his own filth, he looked a healthier colour, pinkish and clean.

Turning the narrow mattress over to the dry side, I laid towels over it, spreading one of his granny's plain white sheets on top and tucking in the edges. It was lumpy but serviceable, and I reckoned it was best to be prepared for more accidents. Finn seemed to have spent any strength he had getting clean; I helped him up and he collapsed on to the narrow bed. Tucking another sheet on top of him, I covered it with all the clean blankets that were left, then began sorting through the stinking mess on the floor. Some of the blankets were probably OK, I thought, or at least usable. I unfolded the heap and began to sift through it.

The last thing I expected to find was what I found. Piss, yes. Shit, yes. But blood? Blood everywhere.

'Oh, God,' I said. 'Oh, God, Finn. What's all this?'

He said nothing, just looked away from me, his eyes brimming with tears, the shadows under them sharply purplish and bruised, his face deathly pale.

153

'Jesus Christ, Finn.' My mind raced. I had no answer for this, for blood. There was so much of it. His face collapsed, he turned away from me and his shoulders began to shake.

'Go away,' he murmured, softly at first, and then louder, shouting, his voice hoarse with pain, 'Go away!'

'Don't worry, *don't worry*.' I was in control. 'I'm going for help!'

I didn't hang around long enough to observe his reaction.

Rule number nine: Don't look back.

26

Even at St Oswald's, that hotbed of cultural mediocrity, every schoolboy knew that the Renaissance was top historical era. It was the age of invention, piety and good government; the age of writing and painting and medicine, of magnificent glittering intellect. You could tick the geniuses off on your fingers: Leonardo, Machiavelli, Galileo, Michelangelo, Shakespeare, Cervantes, Raphael, Gutenberg.

No question about it. The Renaissance ruled.

In our lessons, however, the Dark Ages beat the Renaissance hands down. We didn't care about the Sistine Chapel or the printing press or the flourishing of perspective in art. We cared nothing for the first modern novel or the investigation of anatomy, the invention of the microscope or the discovery that the earth moved round the sun. The rebirth of the classical world was as nothing to us, because like most boys, we were far more interested in blood than in art and culture. We craved beheadings, brutal drawings and quarterings, noses and ears and upper lips cut off for various minor crimes, brandings with hot irons. We longed to hear more of trespassers boiled to death, murderers burnt at the stake, eyes gouged out and tongues pierced through with nails or sliced off at the root. There couldn't be enough rape, pillage, torture, pain, boils, flaying, and stinking festering plague to satisfy our lust for gore.

But then there was Finn, and my first lesson in the difference between what's titillating and what's terrifying, the difference between historical blood and its contemporary equivalent.

When faced with the real thing, real shit, piss, and plague, I did what real heroes never do. I ran. What I required more than anything in the world was my safe little bed in my claustrophobic room, the thick walls and thick attitudes, the meaningless tasks and the trivial rules, the execrable food and the antiquated values and everything else I needed and despised.

It's not that St Oswald's offered comfort. No. It offered certitude. Refuge in the shape of conformity. Deliverance from danger *out there,* a danger I couldn't define, decline, conjugate, calculate.

For a few seconds I *got* it, the meaning of the place.

But it couldn't deliver me from blood.

My head ached. What should I do? In the eyes of the world Finn didn't exist; he had no family, no medical record, no National Insurance number. You couldn't send an ambulance to a beach hut to rescue a non-existent sixteen-year-old and expect no one to ask questions. Perhaps I could beg the school nurse to accompany me to the beach. But no matter how I twisted the players around in my head I couldn't imagine a scenario whereby this could happen.

I arrived panting and desperate back on school property. As I entered the gate, a figure slid out from behind a hedge, silent and boneless, hunched and wringing his hands. I could barely make out his features in the dark, but the posture was unmistakeable.

'What do you want?' I grabbed him by the front of his shirt and pulled him close so I could see the expression on his face. His eyes were round and red with weeping and there were streaks of dirt and tears, and blood.

'Don't, you can't – don't go back to school, they'll, they'll –'

'They'll *what*?'

'I had to tell them,' he moaned. 'They threatened me and –'

'Tell them *what*?'

'Gibbon and and –'

'*Tell them what*?' I shouted in his ear and he winced.

'A-b-b-bout you and the the the . . .'

I threw him to the ground and kicked him in the ribs, though not as hard as I should have. Then I turned my back on his sobbing form and ran. The information didn't particularly ruin my day. So they knew. I'd be expelled, but that seemed like minor news at this particular juncture.

I could see the torches now, patrolling school grounds. Not exactly a threat to a boy in dark clothes on a black night. At the school phone box, grateful for vandals and the smashed light, I dialled emergency services. Gave a false name. Told them there was a boy, ill and bleeding to death, and where to find him. I told them it wasn't a prank call, and how to get to the hut. 'You'll need a boat,' I told them.

'Please stay on the line while we repeat the information back to you,' ordered a voice with sinister neutrality, but I was in enough trouble already, and they'd had plenty of time to get the message.

'I have to go.'

'I'm sorry,' came the monotone, 'but we can't help your friend unless you give us your –'

I hung up.

Then I turned and walked away, ambled actually, calmly, trusting someone else to do what was right. I had done enough, had taken enough responsibility for saving and destroying this particular life.

If I'd been interested in power, of course, the thought might have appealed to me.

27

My two bolt-holes had been closed off. I couldn't go to my room and I couldn't return to the hut. Dodging the torch patrol, I let myself into the school gymnasium through the side door and spent the night hidden at the back of the equipment cupboard. The hard brown vaulting mats made a serviceable mattress; my coat did for a blanket. But dreams tormented my thoughts and it was impossible to sleep. At dawn I walked through the woods at the back of the playing fields, and followed an overgrown footpath the long way round to where it met the coast beyond Finn's island. I approached carefully, aware of Reese's warning, and wondered how specific his confession had been. I had no idea what I'd find.

At the coast, all was silent, but it would be more than an hour before I could cross. So I sat down on the cold sand in a depression surrounded by sea grass, pulled my arms deep into my coat, wrapped my school scarf round my face and waited.

A noise very close woke me and I opened my eyes. Like a nightmare vision, the entire world was blotted out by

Reese's spotty, frightened face. He knelt uneasily, ready to flinch away if I hit him again.

'What are you doing here?'

He said nothing.

'Go. Do you hear me? GO.' I grabbed his hair with one hand and his throat with the other and he rocked backwards, startled and gasping, eyes overflowing with tears.

'I can't go back,' he sobbed. 'I can't. Gibbon says –'

'Oh, fuck Gibbon.' I couldn't even be bothered to shout. I felt sorry for Reese, but there wasn't room in my overcrowded brain for him just now, and probably never would be.

He backed off about fifteen feet and hovered, and I thought *if only I had a rock or a handful of gravel to throw at him*. Instead I closed my eyes, wishing him gone.

The next time I opened them the world was empty, the sky heavy and grey, the sea unnaturally flat. A flicker of movement turned out to be nothing but shivering reeds. In another twenty minutes the causeway would appear, but I already knew the hut was empty. I could taste Finn's absence in the air.

Of course I was right. There was no note. No forwarding address.

I sat down, relieved, my heart hollow. In a trance of habit I banked up what remained of the fire and put the kettle on. Finn's cat rubbed against my legs and I kicked it away. It slid out of range and stood staring at me with its cold yellow eyes, unperturbed by the strength of my dislike.

The thought of returning to school sickened me. There would be a gargantuan uproar when I returned, and somehow I'd have to find Finn. And what would happen when I found him? I gazed up at the sky, wondering if I should just leave town. Exhaustion settled over me, into me, suffused my bones. I was tired of running, needed time to think.

As my tea brewed, the air grew heavier, intensified into an uncomfortable clamminess, and maybe if I'd had access to a newspaper or radio I'd have known what was happening, would have had time to make a plan or batten down the hatches. But as it happened, the first I knew something was wrong was when I saw the wooden foundation of the hut submerged in water. The sea was oddly flat. There was always at least a gentle swell and fall, though more usually little white riffles and uneven waves. It looked eerie out there now, unnatural. Dead flat and motionless.

A concatenation of signs.

I remembered about the sandbags, and with a feeling of resignation, dragged them from behind one of the other huts, wondering whether they should go inside or outside. After some hesitation, I pulled them in over the threshold and slumped them by the door.

An area of light appeared in the sky, sharp as a razor and weirdly dazzling in a way that made no sense if I looked inland past the town, at an ordinary pale blue sky. It was only when I went outside and turned to the north that the strange light made sense. There, a flat greenish-black area of cloud had attached itself to the sky like a malignancy.

It was still a mile away, moving slowly down the coast, the sickening mass boiling slightly. I stood mesmerized, watching the rain stream from it in dark vertical rods. A wall of cold air hit me, so solid I could have reached out and felt its edges. It swept over the beach like a plough, parting the humid air. I could hear the storm right behind it, a wild hissing noise like God calling for quiet, followed by a blaze of branched lightning and a crack of thunder, loud and close. Half a mile up the beach the landscape looked comic, the world turned wrong way round. I could see the tops of scrubby trees bent almost flat as huge waves battered the dunes. The angry, biblical violence that slouched south along the coast couldn't have looked less like the weird calm at my feet. Watching it, I felt the extent of my vulnerability, my laughable, pitiable humanity. When it hit, it would hit like a fist. What power I had once possessed was gone, transported (I hoped) to somewhere safe, and I was left behind, exposed and small, too weak to fight, too slow to run away, with a brain drowning in loneliness and self-doubt, and a poor human voice that could never make itself heard above the crash of the sea, even if there had been someone to listen.

The rain hit. For a moment I stood in the doorway and spread my arms and invited it to drench me, wash the blood from my conscience. But it didn't. It just soaked my clothes, my hair, and my feet, left me shivering with exposure and self-consciousness.

What followed was like no storm I'd ever experienced. The sea lashed at my feet, the wind howled, the lightning and thunder came together in an ecstasy of torment as the sky contracted with one screaming birth spasm after another, pushing out a vile purple beast with an uncontrollable temper.

There was no longer any time to run away, and (in any case) nowhere to go. I slammed the door shut and hauled on shutters stiff and rusted with lack of use, pulling them free, fastening their metal bolts over the window frames. Slamming the final shutter plunged the hut into darkness; the only light dribbled down from the diamond-shaped window in Finn's room, so green and faint I could barely see my shaking hand in front of my face. The little flickering flame of the storm lamp offered light but no comfort. I huddled in a corner.

Outside, something (the wind?) screamed. Once. Twice.

As the minutes ticked by, I lost confidence in my senses. I'd heard that rabbits screamed when their throats were cut.

It came again and it might have been human or it might have been animal but it definitely wasn't the wind. I slipped out of the door into the gale and tried to peer through the sheets of rain, but it was hopeless, the rain so heavy I couldn't see anything at all. Soaked and shivering, slammed by wind and rain, I waited. It came again, only this time more clearly, and I ran towards the sound.

He stood on the shore, across the channel from me, and all I could see of him was an outline. But there was no doubt, it was my rabbit, my Gollum. Reese.

Crystallized to a pinpoint of pure terror, he had become less than human, incapable of rational action. I shouted to him, and only long afterwards realized I might have saved his life by doing nothing at all.

He heard me and waved his arms, dashed up and down the beach in panic, then plunged into the churning water, and it didn't matter what I shouted then because the wind snatched my words away and if he heard anything at all, it would just have been a howl, as human or as inhuman as his. I waded in as far as I dared, my voice hoarse with shouting at him to stop, go back, my usual threats. For a moment I saw his head bobbing as he thrashed against the angry sea, but even the very best swimmer would be helpless in this storm, and Reese was anything but the best.

I stood shoulder-deep in churning water with no strength left to shout or fight against wind and sea, and there was a moment during which I thought I could sink slowly to the bottom where the wind and rain and my thoughts couldn't reach, and there drift slowly, silently into sweet unconscious eternity. The promise of peace extended its arms to me and I swayed softly towards it . . . but . . . no. Whoever decides such things had decided. Life wasn't finished with me yet.

By the time I hauled myself back on to dry land, there was no longer any sign of Reese.

Inside the hut, I stripped off my clothes with awkward fingers, wrapped myself in a blanket and fell asleep, empty and exhausted. Minutes or seconds later the noises in my head jerked me awake, while the gale howled louder than ever and the sea crashed against the hut walls. It was inky dark, the candle flame drowned in a pool of melted wax. I crammed another candle on top of it, grateful to the pinpoint of light and its feeble warmth. It repaid me with treachery, illuminating the sea trickling in through the front wall. I begin clearing things off the floor, mechanically, doing what had to be done.

An hour later, or two, or three, I tried opening the door a crack, but the wind swooped down and stole the handle from my hand with a howl of glee, wrenched the door sideways, and filled the hut with a gale furious enough to send us whirling off to Oz. It took all my strength to pull it shut and it wasn't the wind that frightened me so much as the garish purple-and-yellow sky.

For what seemed an eternity, the storm raged. Now I could hear something banging against the house, repeatedly, BANG BANG BANG, followed by a pause; BANG BANG BANG. I couldn't think what it might be, couldn't know that the metal chimney had blown off (still connected by a single screw along one edge) and was smashing a hole in the roof as it tried to break free and fly away. The entire hut groaned and squealed with anguish, unable to withstand the wild, wild wind. If only I had a radio, or a telephone, or any of the thousand modern devices Finn had scorned in favour of a slow picturesque suicide by the sea. What on earth had made me return to this place? Only a lunatic would choose to live so lightly moored to land with no protection from sea monsters and the wrath of heaven.

Four hours. Five. Six. Snatches of sleep filled with images so horrible it was preferable to stay awake. Gales swept down the ragged hole in the roof where the chimney used to be, spewing damp ash over everything. I began to imagine it was howling at *me*, refusing to stop until the hut had turned me out, turned me over to the forces that would try my case, convict me of murder and treason, sentence me to death.

I began to laugh wildly, realizing with a start that the gale would blow the house down if I didn't do something to stop it. And suddenly I knew exactly what to do. I threw open the door, the shutters, the windows. I filled the house with holes so the wind would pass through instead of flattening it.

Inside became thrilling, a tempest in a teacup. I tried to save what was loose, but it was too late, the wind snatched anything light enough to fly and turned it into a missile, so that after five minutes I gave up, scrambling retreat up the little staircase to safety. Under the eaves the air retained traces of stuffy warmth and I huddled on Finn's bed waiting for it to pass, as all things must do.

The next time I awoke it was quiet. Not just quiet, silent. Still as death.

Wrapped in my cocoon in the dark, I slept again, a mercifully dreamless sleep, waking at dawn to a warm spring day with the sun streaming in the open windows.

The morning was all innocence, as if its night of passion with the storm had never occurred. In the sweet stillness of the day, it seemed to be denying all knowledge of the seaweed, the upturned table, the smashed crockery, the kitchen full of water and sand. *All these things are mysteries*, whispered the soft still air caressingly, *I am not responsible*.

Rule number ten: There is no such thing as truth.

28

All over Finn's tiny kingdom were remnants of the storm, bits of boats, cork, shells I'd never seen before, mounds of seaweed, dead fish – but no body, and I found myself imagining (hoping, praying) that Reese had swum to safety.

I went for help.

There was no official welcome. A notice at the school gate warned *pregnant visitors or those in compromised states of health* to report directly to the head's office. Despite the pleasant morning it was eerily quiet. There was no one about, no movement or sound; the ground was covered with branches and roof tiles swept up and smashed by the storm. A group of third-form boys suddenly materialized from round a corner, skipping across the ground like blown paper. In answer to my cautious query the leader shouted happily that lessons had been cancelled until further notice.

'They're looking for you,' one of them laughed, and I shivered. I must tell someone about Reese. And yet I couldn't, not without turning myself in. Besides, Reese was probably dead and Finn might still be alive. So I walked, stumbled, lurched into town. Waited for a woman with a huge supply of coins to finish an endless conversation of staggering banality, then took her place, closed the door and opened the phone book.

There was only one hospital near St Oswald's. I dialled the number and asked if a haemorrhaging boy with glandular fever had been admitted two nights ago. The woman at reception said no.

'His name is Finn,' I insisted.

'Finn what?'

I had no idea.

'Sorry,' she said, sounding anything but. 'I can't help you without a surname.'

The sound I made was expressive of despair.

'Though as a matter of interest . . .' She sounded kinder now. '. . . I don't see anyone with that name on our admissions list.'

As an afterthought I asked for Reese. Her answer was the same and I put the phone down.

An image arrived unbidden in my brain, of Finn and Reese, pale and cold as marble, stored unclaimed in adjoining refrigerated drawers. The terror lurking just beneath the surface returned, and tears filled my eyes, blinding me. The newsagent on the high street told me where to find a bus to the hospital. I didn't know what I'd do when I arrived.

The hospital looked new and ugly. Low-built and surrounded by car parks, it sprawled across what must recently have been a meadow. Behind the hospital buildings, cows pressed together against wire fencing. It took a minute to find the entrance, hidden among a series of blue and mirrored glass panels, and I wondered whose glaring incompetence had considered this a clever design for the entry to Accident and Emergency. I stepped through the doors that didn't look like doors into a room with a large podium-style island marked *Reception*. To the right I could see the waiting room, in which a handful of broken-limbed or otherwise blighted individuals slumped. A man in his twenties with a congealed cut across one cheek lay asleep in one of the chairs. Another stared blankly at a machine offering *Coffee or Tea. Your Choice!*

'Hello,' I said, leaning over the reception desk in a vain attempt to get a look at the register. 'I'm looking for my friend –'

I paused. And in the instant of that pause, I could picture the scene, could see it happening. When they came for him they'd have asked his name. And I realized that despite his air of mystery I knew him. I knew how his mind worked.

The receptionist appeared indifferent to our relationship, to my motives, to any lie I might be preparing. She searched in her admissions book for the name I gave.

My name.

'Here's your friend,' she said, and inside I shrieked with triumph. 'Admitted on Wednesday. Ward F. The lift is behind you.'

I pushed the button with a wobbly finger.

The matron on duty checked her list. 'Yes,' she said, and pointed. 'In the far corner.' She barely looked up.

I tiptoed down the corridor, desperately needing Finn to

smile at me weakly from deep down in his dark cipher's eyes and thank me for saving his life.

There were eight beds in the room, all occupied. He lay in the corner with his back to me, covers drawn high up around his head.

I approached softly. 'Finn . . .?'

Did he flinch?

I said his name once more, but there was no answer, so I sat on the ugly green chair beside the bed and waited. A different nurse came by to check his blood pressure, take his temperature.

'We're not getting much out of her today,' the nurse told me with a smile.

She, I thought, annoyed. But that always happened with my name. I'd been teased about it, taken for a girl on class registers my entire life.

And yet, I thought, what kind of nurse can't tell the difference between a boy and a girl?

'Is he going to be here much longer?'

She gave me a curious look. 'Have you got the right friend?' I followed her eyes to Finn's left arm, curled over the cotton hospital blanket. It looked oddly fragile and delicate, the blue veins visible just under the skin. I could understand where the misapprehension came from.

She said his name, my name, and I gave a mirthless little laugh. 'It's a common mistake. People often think it's a girl's name.'

The nurse paused. 'There's been some question about next of kin, hasn't there? Locating parents or guardians? Didn't they find her living alone?'

I was beginning to feel uneasy. The warmth I'd felt when I realized Finn had taken my name was beginning to cool as I recognized the implications. The sick boy in this bed was supposed to be me. Eventually someone would trace the name to an NHS number, an address, a family, a school. Perhaps they already had.

The nurse looked closely at my jacket and frowned. 'You're a St Oswald's boy?' My clothes were filthy and crumpled, but perhaps no more than she expected. 'Isn't there a quarantine?' She seemed about to say more, but a bell rang on the ward and she turned to go, looking back once from the door. And me? I was too tired to run, and besides, I'd run out of places to go. A feeling of dread settled somewhere in the region of my small intestine.

I waited. Nurses came and went. I couldn't bring myself to approach Finn again. Inside my head, a single question ran endlessly on a loop: Will someone *please* tell me what is going on? Will someone *please* . . .

A young doctor arrived for rounds. He spent a long time leafing through a folder with my name on it, then turned to me. 'Perhaps you can help me, there seems to be some confusion about her NHS number.'

'He is *not* a girl.' I spoke the phrase in a very quiet voice, afraid to make myself heard.

The young doctor looked down at the chart once more. He frowned. 'It says here she was admitted the day before yesterday, suffering from glandular fever and dehydration.'

The facts as I knew them. 'I found him. I called the police. There was blood . . .'

He looked up, brow furrowed, his expression puzzled, but not unkind. 'The patient was menstruating at the time of admission. Do you understand what that word means?'

A wave of something dark flooded the space behind my eyes.

He continued, peering down once more at the chart. 'Though I'll grant you, something's not right. Damned paperwork.' He flipped the pages back and forth. Looked up again with the resignation of someone accustomed to administrative disorder. 'I'll get someone to sort it out.' He stood up to go. 'Her parents are on their way.'

There was a movement from the bed, and slowly, slowly, Finn turned to face me. I could read a lifetime in his eyes, an explanation, an expression of . . . of what? Gratitude? Regret? But no, it was something else. Amusement almost, mixed with shame, as if he had told a joke that turned out not to be so funny after all. I flailed at the moment, desperate to grasp it, but it faded before I could make sense of it and was gone.

Finn turned away and all of a sudden the hilarity of the situation struck me with force. As I tried to control the rising bubble of hysteria, I wondered whose parents were on the way.

29

A few miles from where Finn's hut sat there had once been a large medieval town, a prosperous community arranged round a C-shaped indentation in the coastline. The town boasted five royal galleons and a perfect calm harbour from which fishermen and traders set off adventuring into the North Sea, returning days or weeks later from what is now Holland and Norway and France, their boats filled with embroidered wool and linen, illuminated vellum, silk cloth, soft worsted wool. Most of their food they grew or raised themselves. It was a time of great prosperity, a mini golden age. But it didn't last.

In 1328, a brutal storm reconfigured the coastline of East Anglia. Huge winds drove the sea crossways against the opening of the land, dredging shingle up from the shallow seabed and hurling it against the coast to wall off the harbour, while at the same time scrabbling away at the cliffs and causing one third of the town to collapse into the sea. What had been an idyllic protected cove was now a saltwater lake, and within a decade, the town of six thousand prosperous souls dwindled to half that number, then a quarter, and so on, until only a handful of farmers remained.

About the same time, the Black Death began its inexorable crawl west through Asia, finally reaching France and crossing the channel to Kent. England played its part in the spread of disease, sending an infected ship from London to Norway, which landed with its entire crew dead or nearly dead, each corpse grotesquely dotted with purple and black swellings. A gang of looters, ignorant of plague, caught the disease from their victims and as a consequence of sudden wealth, travelled up and down the coast spreading infection wherever they went. By the time they themselves succumbed, they had passed the disease to a quarter of Norway's coastal population.

Some historians believe that the movement of plague across Europe forms a convenient division between the medieval world and the Renaissance – quite literally a clean sweep between one era and the next.

I cannot, in all honesty, make this parallel with my own life. Any rebirth I experienced came with agonizing slowness, over decades.

It was many years before I saw Finn again.

I was taken into police custody later that same day, thanks to the information Gibbon and his cohort beat out of poor Reese. At the time, so many questions were asked of me, of my parents and teachers, of the school, of the police and social services. And of Finn, presumably. The simple intimacy of those days at the hut gave rise to scenes of chaos and crisis.

There was an inquest into Reese's death, and another into my relationship with Finn. When the newspapers took up the story, they found me guilty of manslaughter and sexual perversity, among other things. I was also judged by my peers, not as a murderer or a reprobate, but a laughing stock.

Good old Hilary. Guilty as charged.

I was released into the custody of my parents for the duration of the case, nearly two years in all, and was exonerated of all charges in the end. Not responsible for Reese's death. Or for anything else. It took much longer for the shame to dissipate and the desire to see Finn again to surface. The shame interests me now, and I wonder at its power. Where was my guilt except in misapprehension, or is the ignorance of youth shame enough?

There was no question of my remaining at home. I told my parents I was through with education, packed a few belongings and what little money I had into a case and left. And was it my imagination, or were they not entirely unhappy to be rid of me? For what is more repulsive to the respectable English middle class than scandal, failure, the dreaded whiff of perversion?

It didn't take a genius to guess where I went. The gravitational pull was irresistible, and besides, I didn't know anywhere else.

I returned in July and waited as usual for low tide. Even at its lowest, the water now came nearly to my waist. The hut looked intact, but had obviously spent a good deal of the past two years flooded. It stank of seaweed and rot; every surface was stained and covered in mould and mud. I set to work at once. It's not as if I had the money for a flat.

The first night I slept upstairs on Finn's old bed, tossing

and turning until eventually, at around midnight, I moved outside. The air was the temperature of blood and smelled clean and salty, and I lay for a long time looking up at the stars. At dawn I gave up trying to sleep, and began dragging whatever was ruined out of the hut and up on to higher ground, laying out things to dry on the sand.

Clearing the place was drudgery, though not without triumphs. While dragging armfuls of stinking seaweed out to the scrubby dunes I nearly tripped over Finn's kayak, exactly where I'd left it, half-covered in sand and reeds and buried like a relic. But when I dug it out it looked intact, and I kissed its tatty green hull in gratitude.

I worked until mid-morning when hunger overcame any desire to finish the job, then took the kayak across the channel, left it in the old place, and walked into town. Heading straight to the most expensive hotel, I strolled into the dining room without looking left or right and sat down at a large table groaning with leftovers from a family of seven. I greeted the distracted parents, ignored their polite look of non-recognition, and began to help myself. Simple.

Meeting the stares of the uncertain waiters with a confident smile, I stuffed myself on rolls, warm coffee with cream, and the remains of a full cooked breakfast that had only been nibbled by a child. The politeness of the staff, their uncertainty as to whether I belonged (didn't his face look familiar?) spurred me on. I particularly enjoyed an untouched plate of sausages, and couldn't have eaten another bite if I'd tried. So, into a starched white napkin went the leftovers and (thanking the girl on duty) out of the restaurant strolled I, my lunch in a bundle, replete.

Next stop was the local hardware shop, where I bought kerosene, nails and a scrubbing brush. I stuffed it all into a large shopping bag, adding a loaf of bread, some butter and one of those cheap ginger cakes wrapped in greased paper. My bag was awkward to carry, so I took the bus. I looked away as it passed my old school.

The next two weeks followed a reassuringly productive pattern. I knew the breakfast staff at The Ship so well by now that they ignored me. I thanked them by being discreet, tidy, unobtrusive. Some days I got lucky and had leftover bacon and eggs, the rest of the time it was toast and hot tea or coffee. As I ate, I observed the hotel residents – well-dressed middle-aged tourists and school parents who rarely spoke over breakfast. Most looked as if they never spoke to each other over anything else either. It gave me a more objective picture of the sort of people who sent their children to St Oswald's, the ones whose marriages were less than passionate, whose involvement with their children brought the word 'duty' to mind quicker than 'love'. Occasionally there was an outdoorsy dog in tow, a spaniel or an apricot poodle to match mother's hair. These hints expanded my cache of information, helped me imagine the homes they owned and the lives they led, with housekeepers and modern appliances and emotional lives kept well in check.

I had never been so interested in the upper middle classes before. But then, I'd never had a chance to observe them in the wild.

Some days after breakfast I bought materials: paint

brushes, tacks, tools, and other things as they occurred to me. Some days I lugged back a piece of second-hand furniture (a chair, a fold-up table) to replace the smashed or rotten things in the hut. Nothing cost much, and it was satisfying, like playing at having a life. The next flood would happen soon enough and I would have to make my home watertight. Each moment demanded my attention.

Once I'd cleared the rubbish, I scrubbed the house till my hands bled. The sun was bright and strong, and it dried quickly and began to smell of salt and the sea instead of rot. I threw open the windows and only closed them at night to keep the moths out. I didn't light the stove, despite missing hot water for tea, but I knew I'd need a fire soon, when the temperature began to drop. Despite the fact that the salty beach wood burned badly, spitting and sputtering like willow, it was considerably easier than transporting sacks of coal across in the kayak.

There was enough repair work to keep me busy all summer. And although DIY wasn't exactly my speciality, I enjoyed the realization that it was possible. First job was to repair the metal chimney, which made a terrible noise smashing against the roof whenever the wind blew, so I replaced the broken brackets and screwed them down tightly. Next, I built a wall around the outside of the hut with sandbags, three deep. It was exhausting work, filling and arranging all the bags for my rampart, and took the better part of two weeks. By the time I had finished, I realized it probably wouldn't work anyway. I wasn't about to spend another week dismantling it, but its uselessness depressed me.

Replacing window glass required precision and expertise, neither of which I possessed. I bought a knife and had the panes cut and wrapped carefully in brown paper at the town hardware shop. It took nearly a whole frustrating day before I got the hang of chipping out the old putty on one side and replacing it with new in a straight smooth line. A few panes had to be trimmed where the windows had shifted and were no longer square, and in doing this I managed to break all four, despite having in my possession a glass cutter. For the second batch I re-measured precisely and paid extra to have the panes cut into parallelograms.

In preparation for winter I bought a roll of insulating wool and pushed it in between the struts of the unlined roof, securing it with whatever boards I could find from the scrap washed up on the beach. To say my patchwork of wood looked inelegant would be an understatement, but it worked – the August sun streamed in all day and the roof space became hot as a sauna. I knew it would come into its own in colder weather, but in the meantime I began sleeping downstairs again, like in the old days.

The following week I found half a box of the pebbly black asbestos tiles Finn had used to repair the roof. He had carefully wrapped and stashed them under the stairs, and I came across them while searching for tools. It had generally been a dry summer, but when it did rain, I needed every bowl and saucepan in the house to catch the drips. So I balanced on the window sill and heaved the heavy box over on to the roof, forgetting to take account of the scorching hot tin edges that took the place of gutters. Thick bands of burns reminded me of my folly for days afterwards, and I waited for an overcast day to try again. The pitch of the roof was only about twenty degrees, but it was difficult to hold a stable position while hammering (how had Finn managed it so easily?). I knelt carefully, hooked my feet over the ridge, then leant forward to nail down as many tiles as possible before sliding off. My technique wasn't wholly satisfactory, given that in the process of nailing on new tiles, the old ones had a tendency to split, and in the end I just tacked strips of tarpaper over the whole mess. If that wasn't the proper thing to do, you can send me a letter.

So piece by piece, I put the house back together, and when I stepped back to look at it, realized it was more snug and ready for winter than it had been during all the time Finn lived there. This realization startled me; I was not used to thinking of myself as the sort of person who could improve upon his work.

Her work.

I never exactly made a decision about what came next. It came over me slowly, ticking quietly at the back of my consciousness for the longest time before I even noticed it was there. But I was halfway to a decision already, living in the hut, becoming what I loved.

You would think there'd be a rule to go with that thought, but I had run out of rules.

30

I went to see Finn's witch.

Two years is a long time in the life of a teenage boy, but in the life of a market trader it's barely longer than a wink. I had the sense that Finn's witch had been at this game for a few centuries at least and was unlikely to change her ways at such short notice. And sure enough there she was, just as I'd left her, with the same filthy handkerchief knotted round her neck and the same face like a rotten turnip. She gave no obvious sign of welcome as I approached, but I could tell from a certain darting away and back again of the eyes that she recognized me. I wondered if she read the local papers, and then realized she wouldn't have had to: the unofficial version of news travelled from stall to stall, and on a good day moved with a great deal more speed and accuracy than Reuters.

She turned her back on me, but I didn't care. I sat down, pretending to concentrate on something in the distance, watched the action at the next stall, hummed to myself. It took nearly a quarter of an hour for her to establish that I wasn't leaving. She came and sat beside me.

'You're back.'

'Yes.'

She nodded.

I remained silent for the longest time, remembering Finn, practising power. And then, 'I need a job.'

She seemed surprised by this, which in turn surprised me. What's the point of second sight if you can't anticipate the simplest conversations?

'Don't suppose you're much use.'

I faced her. Go on, I thought, have a good look. Not the finest specimen, perhaps. But at least I am what I seem to be.

'Tuesday,' she said, just when we were in danger of moving out of awkward silence into permanent stasis. 'Early.'

'How early?'

'Six.'

Six was fine. A job was a job, I wasn't about to quibble over the hours. I was up at sunrise most mornings anyway.

Today was Saturday, and I counted down the hours till my return. I was sick of stolen breakfasts, and the hotel would soon be replacing its summer staff with locals, whom I guessed would be less welcoming. I was also out of money, would have had to try for a job in town if the witch hadn't offered work. The thought of having to serve St Oswald's boys at the Co-op or fish-and-chip shop made me cringe.

In the event, there were no surprises. Tuesday morning at 6 a.m., Witchy pointed to a pile of boxes in the back of a van, pointed again to an area behind her market stall and left me alone. Couldn't have been easier. I unpacked boxes, stacked them carefully at the front of her stall, ran errands, and by 11 a.m., when she handed me a cup of tea, I could no longer raise my arms above my shoulders.

'This the new boy?' The wizened forty-year-old chain-smoker who sold cheese and sweets and tinned sardines at the next stall checked me out. 'Quite a looker, ent he?' she said, unable to control her mirth. Her name was Alice, and it didn't suit her.

The witch handed me a broom. Highly appropriate, I thought as I swept. At one o'clock, she led me over to the market cafe and waved to the waitress, who brought over two plates of sausage and mash and placed one in front of each of us. It was the first proper meal I'd had in weeks that wasn't breakfast, and she didn't try to tell my fortune. I was grateful and vowed to be less unpleasant for the rest of the day.

The market closed up at three, and all the work I'd done first thing had to be undone in the same order, with everything stacked in the back of the van and the stall dismantled. It struck me as an impossible amount of work for the lazy old stump, and I was surprised she'd had an opening for a dogsbody. Perhaps she'd been holding the position open, knowing I was about to show up and ask for it.

When everything was finished, folded and swept, she reached into the little leather pouch round her waist and handed me six shillings. Enough to buy tea and milk and bread and biscuits, and nails, and an economy packet of minced beef.

'When shall I come back?'

'Tomorrow,' she said, clambering into the cab of her little blue van and slamming the door.

Thirty shillings a week. Ecstasy.

31

As the summer wound down, there was less work to do on the hut, and I spent my free time reading books that I borrowed from the library or bought at the junk shop for a penny. Most of what I read was chosen to impress Finn, whose absence I took to be temporary. Or maybe he had existed so much in my head that when he left, the difference was negligible. The thought that he might return at any moment led me to devise topics of conversation based on my reading. It seemed unlikely, after all, that we would spend time reminiscing. I started with classics like *Moby Dick* and *Treasure Island*, but soon drifted into modern adventure: *Kon Tiki*, *The Wooden Horse*, *The Day of the Triffids*. The recent fiction I read furtively, like pornography, in bed.

Week in, week out, I worked and I lived and I thought about Finn.

But which Finn did I think about? The Finn in my head was strong and fearless. Virile. Male.

I knew nothing about the real one.

And yet I waited for his return, in part because I didn't have a better plan. On the plus side, Finn's witch was a good employer (not that I had anything to compare her with), the work was straightforward, and she paid me for it, which seemed a miracle in itself.

On the minus, my sleep was haunted with drownings, and my house (*my house*) was slowly being reclaimed by the sea.

One day it rained constantly and Witchy sent me home early. I trudged the long road to the coast to save bus fare, turning across the marshes as usual. Now that the hut was inaccessible by foot, my main fear was losing the kayak, so I'd bought a heavy plastic-covered bicycle cable and padlock, looped one end through the ring at the bow and secured it to Finn's rusted old winch. I had unlocked the boat, flipped it right side up and begun dragging it down to the channel when I heard a noise, a low hiss of outrage which caused me to drop it and jump back, dumbstruck as a single grey paw emerged from the bow cabin, followed by a grey head with raked-back eyes, twitching torn ears, a coat of matted fur. And, finally, the strange cartoon tail, held erect.

Finn's cat greeted me (its long-lost friend) disdainfully, and stepped into the centre of the boat, each paw meticulously planted, daring me to reclaim what it obviously considered Finn's property, or perhaps its own. But having lost the need to curry favour with its owner, I was no longer frightened of the beast. Wet and bad-tempered, I hissed back at it, took hold of the boat by the gunnels, tossed it roughly into the channel, hauled myself in, and as an afterthought checked with one hand to see if the creature had retreated under the bulkhead. It sank its teeth into my hand just like in the old days, and I withdrew with a curse, looking round to catch Finn's take on my humiliation.

I paddled up to my (*my*) front door and tethered the boat to the latch. It floated in three inches of water where once it would have sat on dry land.

Let the beast get out by itself, I thought, not interested in risking another attack for its welfare. But it followed me exactly, leaping from deck to threshold, then stepping inside, where it carried out an inspection of the new order, tail slowly sweeping back and forth, as if testing for mines. It even rubbed up against me a few times, establishing ownership. And so I was marked: Property of Finn's Cat.

The creature was obviously not reliant on anyone else for survival. Despite its ragged coat and torn face, no ribs showed. I threw it scraps because it had once belonged to Finn, and also because I was in charge. *Noblesse oblige.* So we were bound together by shared loyalty if nothing else.

Pragmatist that it was, the cat began to follow me the way it had once followed Finn – all the way from the beach into town, parading down the centre of the market at my heels. Alice found this behaviour hilarious. Her stall already had four or five cats prowling about, which made perfect sense, given that her cheese gave off the heady aroma of decay. Mice staggered out of their hiding places like drunken sailors, drawn inexorably towards the stink. When this happened, her cats picked them off one at a time with quick, delicate flicks of the paw. The mice were so intoxicated by rotten cheese, they didn't seem to mind being eaten.

Finn's cat did not join the general game, but remained aloof, waiting for particular handouts from the fishmonger. It seemed quite at home sitting patiently in anticipation of lunch, and I wondered if this were the source of its well-padded figure. It certainly shunned anything so demeaning as catching its meals live.

Despite my understanding that cats groomed themselves, the animal's coat appeared to be matted beyond repair and as I refused to touch it, Alice produced a comb and brushed its fur till it fluffed out, shiny and clean, like sable. The creature looked better, beautiful almost, and it pleased me. It was more flattering to be followed around by a thing of beauty.

We had lots of regulars, and one girl hung around the stall most afternoons. I didn't discourage her, and on our third or fourth encounter we struck up a conversation. She had wonderful coppery eyes and asked if my cat had a name. I yawned, bored and a little annoyed by the subject.

'It's called Beast,' I said, aiming a half-hearted kick, and she frowned.

'Don't do that.'

I shrugged and went back to work, and eventually the girl drifted away. But she came back the next day and the next, and I guessed she was desperate for attention because she not only hung around, but started walking home with me, or as close to home as I'd let her come. She was pretty enough, with long, flat hair parted in the centre and she didn't walk so much as wander. Her features were small and clear, and occasionally I squinted at her, trying to imagine her as a boy.

We reached the place where the tarmac road turned left along the coast and I stopped and told her she couldn't come any further.

'Where on earth do you live?' she asked, but I only gestured vaguely towards the footpath that ran across the marshes and practised my inscrutable smile. I didn't turn round or wave, just left her there, Finn's cat following at my heel. I knew it added to my air of mystery, and for once I felt complicit with the beast.

The girl never tried to follow.

32

There are other things I haven't mentioned. Like Finn turning out to be two years younger than I'd thought, which was all part of the scandal. There were enough *anomalies*, as the court-appointed social worker said, to cause serious concern: a sixteen-year-old boy and a fourteen-year-old girl practically cohabiting over school holidays, the girl dressed as a boy and acting like one, and *Lord knows what else*. Articles of my clothing were found in the hut, and a diary of my movements somehow made its way to the authorities. Poor dead Reese, vigilant to the end.

To me they always said: 'Of course you knew, didn't you?'

They mostly asked this question gently, but with a subtext of incredulity, as if they couldn't get their heads round the possibility that anyone could have been so stupid. This was always the question, phrased in a way that stopped just short of the subject of buggery – or something more conventional than buggery, as it turned out. The whole subject made me feel ashamed and furious but most of all embarrassed for Finn, and what he'd become in everyone's eyes because of me.

What she'd become.

No one knew what to think, least of all me. Could I really have been so naive? Every question held a trap, a sex trap usually, and the real questions weren't voiced. You just had to look at the men (it was usually men), wetting their lips a little, sometimes apologetic, sometimes challenging, sometimes just plain desperate for details. *Did you have sex?* they nearly asked, and *How? What exactly did you do? What was the precise nature of your perversion? I'm afraid we'll require details.* Their eyes begged me for details.

Of course, they had it wrong. I said it again and again, sometimes impatiently, sometimes with calm assurance, sometimes in an explosion of violence, though in fact it didn't matter. No matter what I said, my innocence emerged twisted, looking and sounding like guilt and conforming to everyone's worst fears and dearest desires. They wanted us to be perverts so badly that the truth began to sag. *Just tell us,* they cooed, but underneath lurked the words held in readiness: *faggot, paedo, pervert, deviant,* and best of all, *Public School Boy,* as if (with the right sort of emphasis) no further explanation were necessary.

The authorities located Finn's mother, and I expect the reunion was an emotional one. Note how carefully I have phrased that, in order to leave space for the reality of it, whatever that might have been. I doubt she was glad to see him, but I could be wrong. The newspapers reported that she lived nearby, had a boyfriend and two other children – girls. Whatever else may have been true of her, she didn't want Finn having anything to do with me. As if somehow I had made him what he was, when all I did was come along near the end of the story and trust that Finn had told me the truth.

Reese's body was found three weeks later, washed up on shore a mile or so from the hut. After all the testimony, the suggestive headlines, the pointed fingers, it was ruled an accidental death. He had come looking for me, and, overtaken by the storm, had drowned. It was a good simple explanation, despite everything it left out.

Of course, back then, I still thought of history as a full and frank collection of facts. Now I understand that it is only a story, one of many, or many parts of several different stories – in my case, the one about Goldilocks and the Big Bad Wolf.

Think about history and tell me that I'm wrong.

33

I should have liked this particular story to end with me settled happily ever after in the hut on the island, but it didn't happen. It wasn't long before I had to face the fact that I was living in the sea.

Once the fact became obvious, I packed up and left. There was no point hanging about waiting for floods to sweep away all those lives: Finn's, his gran's, the fisherman from a hundred years ago, the farmer from a thousand, and everyone else in between, including me. The closer Finn's island came to extinction, the more I wandered back in my mind to the lives that came before us, the huts and houses, the remains of animals and clothing, the coins and latrines and cooking pots, the messages from the past left in bones and kitchen dumps. And the people.

Sometimes I thought about the content of those lives, the intangible things that leave no fossils and no marks on history. Would people from the future excavate traces of passion? Of hope, disappointment, despair? Would they discover layers of love and layers of loss? Or would the entire human race end up drowned and forgotten, buried under waves of melting ice, with no one left to dig us up or wonder at what was or what might have been?

Which brings me back to the present, where we have begun to drown in a sea of our own making. Our idyll is gone, squandered on a headlong rush towards the future. Our lives in this fragile place have taken their toll. We have emerged, ragged and ruined, filled with wisdom and regrets that are much too late.

We were wrong about time, wrong to believe it would move forward in an orderly fashion filled with promise and opportunity and progress forever. We know now that time leaps and skids and suddenly stops short, as it will soon for me, as it did once on a day in the middle of the twentieth century when I met the person I wanted to be, and asked him for something to drink.

Despite the fact that Finn never blamed me, I paid my penance into a bank account every month for nearly eighty years. He never thanked me and I never wanted to be thanked, so we were in agreement. For reasons I find hard to explain, even now, I paid it in memory of Reese. There was so much of me in him, and I have often wondered whether he may have been the truer friend.

I am almost a hundred years old; waiting for the end, and thinking about the beginning.

There are things I need to tell you, but would you listen if I told you how quickly time passes?

I know you are unable to imagine this.

Nevertheless, I can tell you that you will awake some day to find that your life has rushed by at a speed at once impossible and cruel. The most intense moments will seem to have occurred only yesterday, and nothing will have erased the pain and pleasure, the impossible intensity of love and its dog-leaping happiness, the bleak blackness of passions unrequited, or unexpressed, or unresolved.

And still the brain continues to yearn, continues to burn, foolishly, with desire. My old man's brain is mocked by a body that still longs to stretch in the sun and form a beautiful shape in someone else's gaze, to lie under a blue sky and dream of helpless, selfless love, to behold itself, illuminated, in the golden light of another's eyes.

Time erodes us all.

The coast is gone now, submerged and continuing to sink. Even dear old St Oswald's has been lost at sea, like my Roman fort. I am pleased to say that I've survived long enough to rejoice, at least, in this small aspect of hope amidst our disaster, at the drowning of those mean little classrooms, those mean little aspirations, that mean little history. I have one goal left in life, and that requires me to row my boat over what is left of those towers.

So this is where my story ends. Here, bobbing quietly in a reliable little skiff over the past. I am an old man with a head full of memories, and there is always a part of me that looks backwards, that flows in reverse past the twentieth century, past the nineteenth, eighteenth and seventeenth centuries, and keeps on flying backwards, back, back and further still, until it slows, and finally stops in the middle of the seventh century where I live in a hut by the sea and fish for a living and make stew in an iron pot and collect wood for my fire on the beach and fish and fight in wars to protect what is mine, despite that not being very much.

For many years we had an arrangement. I travelled to see Finn, self-contained and poised as ever, with the same rare smile, still with short hair like a boy's. She always welcomed me gladly, a little absently, secure in my affections while offering only the smallest sliver of herself in return. And what would be different about that?

Sometimes the softness of her eyes and mouth made me wonder how I ever missed the truth about what she was. Though to be fair, she was never anything more nor less than she always had been.

The door was never locked and I was the one who put the kettle on, stirred the tea, fetched the biscuits and laid them on a plate. She was often busy in the garden, and wouldn't come in to me at once.

When eventually we sat down together, she would look at me with the same amused affection as ever, and allow me to gaze into her grave dark eyes and once again feel the familiar tug at my heart. She always asked how I was, and I never once, in all those years, told the truth.

I smile now, knowing that this is all in the past, that I have outlived her; that the story is finished and can never change. I am the only person left on earth with memories of what happened between us and what didn't.

The girl I met at the market came back into my life a few years later. She had cut her hair to shoulder length and I barely recognized her until I saw those coppery cat's eyes.

She tapped me on the shoulder in the queue for the bakery, and we chatted about the weather and the bread and Finn's cat, who still lived with me, and still followed me around in its imperious way.

'I'm Lara,' she told me, and held out her hand.

'My name is Finn,' I told her. It was the only time I said it out loud.

34

Years later I asked another woman to marry me, but she turned me down, not unkindly, merely wanting something more than I could offer. I never asked again, but my life was not empty of incident or affection, which I sought where I could find it, like a man seeks food who has been starved at an early age. I have written books about the coastline, great texts filled with geological observations, meticulously researched and recorded in case some day somebody might care. When I die they will call my contribution invaluable, but my books will slowly fade into history and eventually my life story will be written, if at all, by someone like me who occasionally thinks about such things.

You will have to excuse an old man for conduct you may consider sentimental, but I have made my point and now have a job to do. It is one that I do not with joy or sadness, but resolve.

I am not where I need to be yet, and will not pretend that I have managed to row row row this boat all on my own. My strong and capable boatswain, the godson whom I have loved as a son and who never knew the coast as it was then, follows my trembling finger with great patience as I point and look for landmarks that no longer exist, and estimate distances and study the map, and search for a marker.

Do I sense his relief, now, that my story is done?

What I seek is a Gothic tower, collapsed now. And there, I've found it! Just the base, more or less where I expected it to be. This way, I tell my patient boy (who is no longer a boy, and no doubt thinks me mad), out of the school gate turn right and row along the path just here, now right again that we've come to the dunes. He pulls hard on the oars and looks at me fondly and moves as I direct him, over the featureless sea where once upon a time there was an island, and once upon a time there was a boy who lived on that island, and once upon a time I was young.

And here (approximately, though something in me says *here*) is where we stop for a moment, while I throw a handful or two of dust and bone into the wind and say a prayer to the spirit of the sea and sky. And in my prayer (which I pray silently, so as to embarrass neither of us) I give thanks for all that has passed, and all that is passing, and all that is yet to come.